Child of the Wolves

OTHER YEARLING BOOKS YOU WILL ENJOY:

VENUS AMONG THE FISHES, *Elizabeth Hall and Scott O'Dell*
THUNDER ROLLING IN THE MOUNTAINS, *Scott O'Dell and Elizabeth Hall*
ISLAND OF THE BLUE DOLPHINS, *Scott O'Dell*
ZIA, *Scott O'Dell*
MY NAME IS NOT ANGELICA, *Scott O'Dell*
THE BLACK PEARL, *Scott O'Dell*
SHILOH, *Phyllis Reynolds Naylor*
THE GRAND ESCAPE, *Phyllis Reynolds Naylor*
MR. TUCKET, *Gary Paulsen*
CALL ME FRANCIS TUCKET, *Gary Paulsen*

YEARLING BOOKS are designed especially to entertain and enlighten young people. Patricia Reilly Giff, consultant to this series, received her bachelor's degree from Marymount College and a master's degree in history from St. John's University. She holds a Professional Diploma in Reading and a Doctorate of Humane Letters from Hofstra University. She was a teacher and reading consultant for many years, and is the author of numerous books for young readers.

Child of the Wolves

Elizabeth Hall

A Yearling Book

Published by
Bantam Doubleday Dell Books for Young Readers
a division of
Bantam Doubleday Dell Publishing Group, Inc.
1540 Broadway
New York, New York 10036

ISBN: 0-440-41321-4

Reprinted by arrangement with Houghton Mifflin Company

Printed in the United States of America

December 1997

10 9 8 7 6 5 4 3 2 1

OPM

For Lauren
and to Nylak

Contents

Author's Note

This story was inspired by Nylak, my Siberian husky. As I watched her grow, I noted the wolflike nature of some of her behavior. This led me to wonder if wolves and dogs could learn to live together peaceably. At the time, biologists saw wolves and dogs as separate species, classifying wolves as *Canis lupus* and dogs as *Canis familiaris,* making the prospect unlikely. Then in 1993, the notion of their similarity received support. Armed with evidence from molecular genetic analysis, biologists decided that dogs were actually a variety of wolf and called them both *Canis lupus.* Each animal, however, received its own name — *Canis lupus lupus* for the wolf and *Canis lupus familiaris* for the dog.

The more I learned about dogs and wolves, the higher rose my respect for their intelligence. Biologists once believed that only human beings had thoughts or emotions. Given what animals regularly do — from learning by observation and using tools to communicating symbolically — it seems odd that the notion was ever accepted. As Elizabeth Marshall Thomas wrote in *The Hidden Life of Dogs,* "The general assumption that other creatures lack consciousness is astonishing."

Animals feel emotions once regarded as strictly "human," and they can learn, think, and solve problems. If wolves were not intelligent problem solvers, they would be unable to cope with dilemmas and could never survive in the wild. The wolf pack is a highly developed social system, which depends on communication among the pack members as well as between separate packs.

Without the pioneering research of biologists Adolph Murie and David Mech, we would know little about the ways of wolves. The intelligence, curiosity, playfulness, social life, and personalities of these creatures shine through their work. *A Child of the Wolves* would be merely musings were it not for Murie's *The Wolves of Mount McKinley* and *A Naturalist in Alaska;* Mech's comprehensive classic, *The Wolf;* and *The Arctic Wolf,* his book on the white wolves of Ellesmere Island. *White Wolf,* the National Geographic videotape of that pack (photographed by Jim Brandenburg), shows Mech's wolves in action, and Brandenburg's own book about the pack, *White Wolf: Living with an Arctic Legend,* describes the same wolves from a different perspective. Nearly as essential to the story were my stay at the Denali Foundation in Alaska and my time at the International Wolf Center in Ely, Minnesota, an organization founded by Mech, which publishes the valuable journal, *International Wolf.* The book's final shape is in good part due to careful readings of an early draft by Dorothy Markinko and Renee Cho.

Child of the Wolves

1. The Beginning

Snow fell for three days without stopping. Drifts collected in the corners and covered the fences. It was the middle of April, but winter still gripped this corner of Alaska west of Cook Inlet. A bitter wind blew across the lake and whipped through the trees, driving the snow into every crack and crevice. Since dawn, Seppala had been moving restlessly in her snug wooden house. Now she began to strain, stopping to pant after every push. It was at least an hour before anything happened.

Then, after an extra-hard push, a small wet bundle slid out onto the straw between her legs. Seppala tucked her head under her raised thigh. With strokes of her rough tongue and delicate nibbles of her sharp teeth, she stripped away the thin membrane surrounding the bundle.

The bundle, which weighed no more than a pound, stirred, then cried out.

Seppala chewed through the connecting cord. She licked the bundle clean and dry, and nudged it to her side.

The newborn puppy could not see or hear. It nuzzled its mother's belly, blundered onto a nipple, and began to nurse. Seppala curled around her puppy and rested.

The wind howled around the edges of the roof, rattling a loose shingle. Bracing herself, Seppala strained again. Soon there was a second furry packet in the straw, then a third. By midday, the snow stopped, the air was calm, and four Siberian husky puppies slept at her side.

Across the yard came a man and woman, their snowshoes leaving tracks in the soft snow. They opened the gate and walked across the pen to the doghouse. The woman fell to her knees.

"Look! Seppala's had her puppies. Four of them!" Kate stroked the dog's head. Seppala raised her head and licked Kate's hand. "Good girl! They're beautiful—just like you."

The man leaned over the pups. He inspected each one. "Three males and a female," Tim said, "and healthy. They're racing dogs for sure."

2. *Granite*

For two weeks the puppies lived in a place of darkness and silence. Their world was small, no larger than the feel of a rough tongue stroking the fur on their bellies and the taste of warm milk.

Then Granite's eyes opened for the first time. Light streamed in, and slowly the blurry world took shape. He was nestled between his mother's paws, looking up at her face. When Seppala noticed his gaze, her own blue eyes widened and she growled softly with satisfaction, then licked the nose of her first-born.

When Granite raised his head and looked out, he saw snow falling silently over a white land. As far as he could see, there was nothing but snow and spruce trees, their dark branches heavy with great, fat flakes. Nestled beside him in the straw were his sister and brothers, all fast asleep.

Seppala licked Granite's face again. It made him feel warm and happy.

Another week passed, and sounds entered Granite's world. The rustle of straw, the squeals of his litter mates, the calls of birds. About this time, the puppy pulled his front paws under him and pushed. Suddenly he was standing shakily on his front feet, sniffing the air. A strange smell filled his head. It was sharp but not unpleasant. Before he could trace the smell to its source, he collapsed in a heap. The smell got stronger.

A large hand swooped down and lifted him up. Granite yelped and squirmed, but it did no good. He was held tight. A growl rumbled deep in Seppala's throat, and Granite's heart beat fast.

The commotion woke the other puppies, who began whining and nuzzling Seppala's belly. As soon as their mouths brushed a nipple, they fell silent and began sucking.

Tim inspected Granite, who did not know whether to relax or bite the stranger. When the pup twisted, Tim spoke gently. The rumbling sounds that came out sounded friendly. Then he turned Granite about and put him back beside Seppala. Her tongue washed the strange scent from Granite's fur and he felt safe again.

He looked at his brothers and sister, but they had fallen asleep again. Once more he stood up. This time his legs were stronger. He staggered across the straw to the edge of the box and watched the creature that had picked him up become a blur in the snow.

Before many days passed, Granite learned that these giant creatures cared for all the dogs in the kennel. At least thirty dogs lived in pens that stretched far across the flatland, nearly to the edge of the forest.

As far as Granite was concerned, the humans belonged to the dogs. He watched them bring food, clean pens, and strew fresh straw in the sleeping boxes. Then they disappeared, only to return whenever a dog needed them.

Around the dogs' kennels was a wire fence that protected the pups from the strange creatures that lived in the woods. Granite had never seen most of these animals, but when the sun was gone and the world turned black, he could hear the sounds they made as they searched for food. Already he knew the strong scent of the red fox, who prowled nearby each night, the tip of its tail waving white in the darkness. Another familiar scent was the spicy smell of the spruce squirrel, who chattered at the dogs from high branches.

The other puppies paid no more attention to the fence than did Granite. They spent most of their days tumbling about, chewing on sticks and rocks and each other. Sometimes they got so tired that they fell asleep in the middle of their games, too weary to scramble into the box and curl up beside their mother.

At other times life was too exciting for sleep. Each morning when the kennel work was done, one of the humans harnessed some of the big dogs to a sled. When the dogs heard the shout, "Hieek! Go get 'em!" they started to run. Off they went across the frozen lake, the runners skimming over the ice. The sight made Seppala whine with longing, for she was a racing dog, like the rest of them.

Granite thought that his mother was beautiful. Her body and head were a silver gray, but like the insides of her sharp ears, her forehead and muzzle were white. Above her eyes ran a strip of tan, outlined in black. Her ice-blue eyes, rimmed in black, were shadowed by long, white lashes. Her white tail was long and bushy, and it rose high in the air, then curled over and rested on her back.

Granite, his brother Nugget, and his sister Cricket looked like their mother. But his brother

Digger, who was the biggest pup of all, was black where Seppala was gray, and the white blaze on his forehead was narrow, instead of wide like hers.

Each time a sled came out of the storehouse, Digger, Nugget, and Cricket lined up at the fence, yelping with excitement. Granite didn't yelp at all. In silence, he watched the big dogs pulling the sled and going where the lead dog took them. Then he left his noisy brothers and sister and raced through the kennel yard, going wherever the world's delicious smells lured him.

3. Something Goes Wrong

Wisps of clouds sailed across the sky. The sun warmed the earth. Between the kennels and the trees, the ground was green with new grass. A narrow strip of ice along the edge of the lake had melted and black water stretched its fingers from the shore. The sleds were put away, and the dogs now pulled a three-wheeled cart among the tall trees, along winding trails. The puppies were four weeks old.

Early one morning, Kate took them out of the pen. A slight breeze ruffled the new leaves. A bird with a bright red head started a noisy chatter. Granite sniffed the air and caught the scent of spruce squirrel and moose. He rolled in the grass and stretched his legs.

Digger ran at Granite and put his forepaws over his brother's neck. With a growl, he stood on his hind legs and pushed, trying to throw Granite to the ground. Granite growled back to show that Digger was not the boss. The growl didn't stop Digger. He fastened his sharp milk teeth into his brother's back. Granite yelped with pain and shook him off.

The pups tumbled over and over, but neither was able to grab the other. Finally, Granite wriggled free and stood up. He put his paws on Digger's neck, pushed him flat, and gave him a sharp bite. Digger yelped and rolled over on his back.

Granite yipped in satisfaction. Digger could make Nugget and Cricket roll over and whimper, but Granite never gave in. He fought back every time.

Disgusted, Digger got up and shook himself. He ran over to where Nugget, the runt of the litter, was sunning himself on the grass. As soon as Digger growled and nipped his neck, Nugget rolled onto his back. Digger then marched off with his tail in the air.

Kate knelt beside Granite, who was watching his brothers. He held up his head to be stroked. But instead of fondling the little dog, she pulled a harness over his head. Granite fought hard and nipped at her fingers, but it was no use. She placed the straps across his back, buckled them around his belly, and snapped on a lead. Then she put him down and stepped back a few paces.

"Come, Granite!" she called. "Come!"

Granite wasn't sure what he was supposed to do. He took a step forward and stopped. Something was dragging behind him. The lead was fastened to a flake of hay. He bit on the lead, trying to chew it in two.

Kate stopped him. "No!" she shouted. "Come!" She made encouraging sounds.

Granite took a step.

"Good boy!" she said. It was the kind of sound she made when she was pleased.

Granite looked at her. He decided that if he went to her, she might pet him and take off the bulky gear. He took another step, even though he didn't like the tug of the strap across his chest. As he walked toward Kate, the hunk of hay bumped across the ground.

When Granite reached her, she said "Good boy!" again and scratched him under the chin. That felt good. Then she gave him a bite of meat. That tasted even better.

Kate stepped back again. "Come, Granite!"

This time the pup trotted over fast.

"Good boy!" she said, and gave him another scratch and another morsel of meat.

Granite wagged his tail. He was ready to run to Kate as long as she fed him. At least until he was full.

But before Granite had all the meat he wanted, Kate unhitched him and put the harness on Digger. The big pup squirmed so hard that she had trouble guiding the strap into the buckle.

One after another, Digger, Cricket, and Nugget bounced across the grass, their tails held high in the air, their necks arched proudly. They strutted like lead dogs. They would have pulled hay all day without a single bite of meat.

Granite looked on in silence. He would work only as long as he was hungry.

After the lesson, Kate carried the pups back to the pen. They ran to Seppala. She was not waiting at the fence, but lay inside the big box, stretched out on her side. She didn't even raise her head to greet her eager children.

Granite sniffed at his mother's mouth and nuzzled her neck. She whined but did not lick his nose as she always did. On this day there were no welcoming caresses. Something was wrong. Fear flowed through Granite, but he did not know why.

Kate noticed that Seppala was acting strange. She made concerned sounds and knelt at Seppala's side. With gentle fingers, Kate pressed the dog's neck, then ran her hand along the dog's belly. She looked into her eyes and mouth. Kate shook her head. Seppala was sick.

The puppies were so upset by their mother's stillness that they forgot to fight. They huddled against the wall and whimpered.

Kate called out. Tim came over from another pen, holding a pitchfork.

"Look at Seppala," said Kate. "I don't know what's wrong, but she's too ill to be nursing puppies. They'll drain her strength."

Tim shook his head. "You've got to think about the pups, too," he said. "They might pick up whatever Seppala has."

The sounds they made were so unhappy that even Granite could tell they were worried.

"We'd better take the pups into the house where we can care for them," said Kate.

"Guess so," said Tim. He sighed and put down his pitchfork. He squatted beside the pups and picked up Nugget, then Digger. He walked toward the house, carrying one in each hand.

Kate made soothing sounds and rubbed Seppala's head. The dog whined softly.

Kate tucked Granite in one arm and Cricket in the other. "It's okay, guys," she said. "You'll be fine and so will your mom."

The sounds were cheerful, but Granite could tell she was not happy. As she carried the pups off, Granite looked back over Kate's shoulder at his mother. Too sick to object, she did not move.

4. Life in the Humans' Box

The human box puzzled Granite. There was no straw inside it. It was enormous, with solid walls and a smooth, shiny floor. The walls were many puppy leaps apart, and the floor was so slippery that his claws skittered across it. Each time Granite tried to walk, he fell on his face. He yelped, but nothing happened. He yelped again.

Kate heard his cries and pushed a gray box with a wire gate into a corner of the room. She dropped the pups into the box and fastened the gate. The floor was strewn with fresh straw. The close walls made Granite and Digger feel safer, but Nugget and Cricket began to cry.

Granite licked Cricket's and Nugget's noses to comfort them, but he still felt bad inside. He longed to be back in the kennel, curled up beside Seppala's warm body.

After a time, the whimpers stopped. The room grew quiet. Then Digger got up and began to chew on the gate. To get his teeth around the wire, he had to draw back his lips. He looked so funny that Kate laughed.

The door banged and the pups were alone. Granite kept watch for the humans, but it was so warm that his eyes kept closing. Before long he was fast asleep.

The sound of boots on the shiny floor woke him up. Digger was standing at the gate whining softly. Nugget and Cricket were still asleep. Granite smelled warm milk and his heart gave a little leap. He looked around for Seppala, but saw only the broad stretch of floor and Kate's legs in blue jeans.

"Time for dinner!" she announced. "Maybe a bottle will make you babies feel better." She opened the gate and pulled Digger into her lap.

Granite peered through the wire and watched her stick a nipple into his brother's mouth. The nipple was attached to a bottle filled with milk. First Digger tried to chew on it, then some of the milk dripped onto his tongue. He began to suck greedily and soon emptied the bottle.

When it was Granite's turn, he knew what to do. As the warm milk ran into his mouth, he swallowed as fast as he could. Kate's arm was around him, and she held him close. Granite felt safe again, but still longed for his mother.

After Cricket and Nugget ate, Kate left. It grew dark. Granite put his muzzle on Cricket's shoulder and tucked his feet into the warmth beneath Digger's belly. Nugget whimpered and scooted as close to the other pups as he could. For a time, they slept.

The next morning, the pups ate oatmeal mixed with eggs, honey, meat, and milk. It tasted good and warmed their stomachs, but it was not the same. They missed being held close. When the oatmeal was gone, the pups went out to practice pulling hay.

It was a soft spring day. With a flash of yellow, a small bird flitted overhead and perched on a willow bush. A squirrel ran up a large spruce tree. Across the lake, a mother caribou picked her way down to the water, her newborn calf trailing behind her.

Kate knelt to put a harness on Digger. Her back was toward Granite. He slipped away and ran for the kennels, as fast as he could go. All the pens looked alike. He couldn't tell which one held his mother. Down the row he ran, yelping for Seppala. A dog answered his cries, but it was not his mother.

Granite rounded the corner and ran square into Tim. The pup tumbled head over heels. It knocked the breath out of him. Before he could get on his feet, Tim grabbed him.

The pup squealed and tried to squirm out of Tim's grasp, but his hands were big and strong. He tried to nip Tim's fingers, but Tim only laughed.

"Where do you think you're going?" he boomed. "I'll bet you're looking for Seppala. Poor little lonesome pup."

Tim carried Granite halfway down the pens and held him so he could see inside. Seppala was curled up in her box, fast asleep.

Granite yelped, making as much noise as he could. He wanted to be next to his mother.

One eye opened, but Seppala didn't raise her head. She sighed and closed her eye.

As he petted Granite, Tim made soft sounds. He could tell that the pup wanted his mother.

Granite quieted and licked Tim's hand.

"Satisfied?" said Tim. Then he took Granite back to the other pups and helped harness him for the hay pull.

A gray jay glided onto a nearby branch. It tilted its white head to one side and watched closely as Granite trotted from one human to the other.

"Whee-ah! Whee-ah!" it called as Kate handed over a morsel of meat.

"Be careful," called Tim. "That camp robber has its eye on the meat."

"There's plenty to spare," said Kate and tossed a piece out on the grass.

The jay peered at the meat and squawked again. Then, as Kate turned away to snap the lead on Granite's harness, it swooped down, snatched the meat, and was gone in an instant.

After the lessons, the pups went back to their cage. That afternoon Tim and Kate put a low fence in one corner of the kitchen, where the pups could scamper about and roll in the straw.

Before they left, Tim dropped a thick knot of rope inside the fence. The pups fought over who would play with it. Digger grabbed one end and Granite fastened his teeth in the other. Digger pulled, but Granite pulled just as hard. Granite braced himself with his front paws and jerked hard just as Digger relaxed his grip. Granite tumbled back and found himself staring at the ceiling. He yelped happily and shook the rope. Digger raced over and grabbed the rope again and another game began.

Only Nugget refused to play tug-of-war. He was

so small that he could never win. Nugget's favorite toy was the water pan, which no one tried to take away. He liked to dabble his paws in the water and shove the pan with his nose. Nugget's water game ended when the pan overturned and water spread across the floor. Each time Kate found the empty pan and the puddles, she made unhappy sounds.

The days passed. Before long the pups were pulling twice as much hay. Granite didn't enjoy it, but it made Kate and Tim so happy that he worked as hard as Digger and Cricket.

All the pups missed their mother. Nugget cried himself to sleep every night. Granite felt like it, but choked back the whimpers. Instead, he tried to comfort Nugget and Cricket. Digger never cried, but sometimes stood sadly at the fence, his head hanging so low it touched the straw.

The morning the pups had their first meal of kibble, they left the big house. After lessons, they went back to the kennel. Seppala waited for them, running back and forth behind the gate and whining. She was thin, but her welcoming bark was as loud as ever.

Tim opened the gate and the pups ran to her. In their eagerness, Cricket and Nugget and Granite tumbled over their feet. Haughty Digger brought up the rear. Seppala licked their noses, sending messages of love. Then she caught Tim's gaze and scolded him for keeping her children so long. He seemed to understand her howls and barks, because he apologized.

After he left, Seppala bathed each pup, washing the human smell off their fur. When she ran her tongue over him, Digger forgot his pride and whimpered like a tiny puppy.

By the time the pups began to play, Digger's pride was restored. He bounced across the ground and leaped on Granite, pushing him flat. Granite was so happy to be back with his mother that he paid no attention. Instead of scrambling to his feet, Granite let Digger hold him down. Digger's blue eyes sparkled and he strutted around the yard, holding his tail like a banner. He strutted until the pups snuggled up beside Seppala for their best sleep in weeks.

5. *The Sale*

Spring moved into summer. Leaves covered cottonwood and willow. Blueberry blossoms dropped, making way for the ripening fruit. Lacy ferns grew among the trees. Pink moss flowers and pale yellow poppies carpeted the ground. Fireweed bloomed, painting the slopes with patches of bright pink. The lake sparkled blue under the July sun. Geese swam in lazy circles and ducks fed along the shore.

Darkness had left the land, taking the stars with it. Every day the sun dipped below the horizon, leaving a world of twilight and shadow, but soon it returned. The sky was never black.

The puppies now ran clipped to a tow line, through a trail cut in the tall grass. Kate or Tom raced behind them, holding the line taut. The pups had learned the trail commands: "gee" for right, "haw" for left, "whoa" for stop.

On one morning when gray skies smothered the sun, no one raced. Rain fell steadily. Water streamed off the roof and pooled in all the hollows.

About noon a truck jolted along the narrow lane that led to the kennels. It stopped in front of the house and a man climbed out. He spoke briefly to Tim and together they walked toward Seppala's pen.

The pups were chasing one another, splashing through puddles. At the sight of Tim, they forgot their game and ran to the fence. With excited yips, they stood on their hind legs, resting their front paws on the wire mesh.

Tim opened the gate and the men walked in. The stranger picked up the pups, one at a time, and looked them over carefully. He opened their mouths, ran his hands down their legs, and turned over their paws, inspecting the pads. He felt their shoulder blades. He even lifted their tails.

The man put Digger down on the ground and ran a hand along his back.

"That one's not for sale," said Tim. "We figure to keep him."

The man backed away and tugged at his beard. The rain dripped off his cap. "You know a good animal when you see one," he said.

"Digger's got the makings of a lead dog."

The man snorted. "How can you tell about a ten-week-old pup?"

"I've got a feel. He's big and tough and he loves to race. Look at the way his bones and muscles are put together. Full chest, long back, long thighs, and short hocks. See the slope of his shoulders and the reach in his upper arms. He'll be a winner, like his father."

The man sighed. He looked at the other pups, then cleared his throat. "All the rest for sale?"

"Sure," said Tim. "Take any of the others. Four hundred fifty dollars."

The stranger made an odd sound in his throat, then picked up Cricket. After inspecting the pup's teeth, the man set the pup down and stared at her. There was a long silence.

The stranger made up his mind. He pulled out his wallet and said, "She's got good lines. Might make a good swing dog—and she'll have some fine pups down the road. I'll take her."

The men shook hands. With the stranger carrying Cricket, they left the kennel and walked through the rain toward the house.

Before long the rain stopped. A narrow beam of sunlight broke through the clouds. Granite stood patiently at the fence, waiting for his sister. He did not understand why the stranger had carried Cricket away, but he was sure that she would be back soon.

A robin dropped to the ground inside the fence. As it hopped along, it turned its head to the side, its yellow eye inspecting the earth for worms. Each hop took it closer to Granite.

Entranced by the bird, the pup left the fence. He stood still, hoping the bird would not notice him. As it came close, he tensed his muscles and sprang. The bird was too quick. With a loud "tyeep!" it flew over the fence. Disappointed, Granite watched the bird fly toward a tall tree. He was so absorbed that he did not hear the approaching footsteps or the sound of the gate.

Without a word, Tim picked him off the ground. Startled, he looked up. Beside Tim stood the stranger, but without Cricket.

When Granite did not see his sister, he felt a prickle of danger. He pushed his nose beneath Tim's arm, making himself as small as possible.

It did no good. Tim pulled Granite out of his hiding place and thrust the puppy toward the stranger.

The man's hand stretched out to receive him. Granite could not breathe. His chest was tight. It felt as if Shadow, the big lead dog, were sitting on it.

The stranger grasped Granite firmly and brought the pup's face level with his own. The man's face was covered with a heavy black beard, which trapped the odor of his last meal. Over the scent of human males and of Cricket, Granite could smell other dogs. He waited, afraid of the man's next move.

The stranger set Granite on a heap of straw and stepped back to see his lines. Granite's head hung low, his ears drooped, and his tail fell between his legs.

The two men began to talk. At first the stranger was hesitant. "He's smaller than his brother," he said. He felt Granite's shoulders. "There's no guarantee that he'll have the strength I want."

"I can't swear he'll be a lead dog," Tim said, "but I know he'll be a credit to any racing team. Racing's in his blood."

The stranger dropped to his knees and again felt Granite's back and legs. He made a series of small, quiet sounds, then got to his feet.

Granite couldn't understand what the men were saying, but when he heard the sound "Granite" come from the stranger's mouth, his ears stood up. He looked at the stranger, then at Tim, puzzled. Neither glanced at him.

He watched as the stranger ducked his head once and grasped Tim's hand. That was what they had done before the stranger carried Cricket away.

Granite did not wait. Before anyone could grab him, he bolted. He ran to the doghouse, where Seppala was curled up on dry straw, and huddled next to her. Then he whimpered.

Seppala seemed to know that something was wrong. She whined as she bathed him, each stroke of her tongue a loving caress.

Granite stopped whimpering, but he was still afraid. He didn't want to leave his mother and Nugget. He didn't want to leave Kate and Tim. He didn't even want to leave Digger. But he could think of nothing to do.

Tim pulled Granite away from his mother. Granite looked about but saw no way to escape. His stomach felt full of stones.

The stranger took the pup and left the kennel. Granite looked over his shoulder and saw Digger and Nugget standing at the fence. Their tails dragged and they looked sad.

As the stranger passed the house, the door flew open and Kate ran out. She called, and the man stopped. Taking Granite in her arms, she held him close and petted him.

The little dog's heart lifted. He knew that Kate would not let the man take him away. She would always protect him. Granite nestled next to her heart, waiting for the stranger to leave.

Kate whispered softly to the puppy. He stretched up and, with the tips of his teeth, gently nibbled the edge of her ear to let her know how happy he felt. She stroked Granite again. A tear rolled down her cheek. Granite licked it off. Suddenly Kate thrust him toward the stranger and turned away.

The stones in Granite's stomach churned. He trembled. He couldn't understand how Kate could let a stranger take him.

The man carried Granite to his truck. It was like the one Tim used to haul dogs to races. Behind the cab were two rows of small doors. In the center of each door was a round hole. Cricket's head stuck out of one hole. She yipped a welcome.

The stranger opened the door next to Cricket. From inside came an old smell of other dogs. The man started to put Granite into the opening.

The puppy struggled, but the man did not let go. He held Granite so tightly that his fingers jabbed into the little dog's body. He thrust Granite toward the dark cavity.

The puppy was desperate. He looked around,

but there was no one to help him. In a panic, he sank his teeth into the stranger's hand and bit as hard as he could.

The man howled with pain and pulled back. Swearing, he jerked his hand to his mouth. Daylight opened beneath his arm.

Granite squirmed past the door and through the narrow space under the stranger's arm. The man grabbed at him, but the hand seized air. Granite jumped to the ground, darted around the back of the truck, and ran into the trees. As he sprinted through rain-soaked ferns, he could hear angry shouts.

6. *Alone in the Forest*

Granite ran and ran and ran. He ran deep into the forest, far from any trail. The voices faded and disappeared. Still the puppy ran. He crashed through ferns and bumped against bushes, sending showers of water from the wet branches. He ran until he could go no farther. His breath came in great heaves. Tired, he sprawled beneath a tall tree. Soon he was fast asleep.

When he opened his eyes, it was twilight. He lay on a patch of ground covered with moss and spruce needles. Through the gloom, he could see the woods stretching forever in all directions. He had no idea where the kennels were. He was lost.

Granite had never been alone before. It was a strange feeling. Pictures of his brothers went through his head. Back in the pens, Nugget and Digger were tumbling in the sweet-smelling straw.

Maybe they were napping, snuggled next to Seppala, their bellies full of warm kibble and gravy. The thought made him sad.

His mouth was dry, but there was no pan of water. Slowly, he got to his feet and stretched. He threw back his head, pointed his nose at the treetops, and sniffed. He turned his head and sniffed again. From a distance came the faint smell of water.

Granite followed the scent through the trees. He heard the sound of a stream. Soon he stood in the shallows, lapping the cool water.

With his thirst quenched, he began to play. He splashed downstream, jumping out to chase spotted wood frogs as they bedded down for the night. When he tired of his game, he trotted beside the rushing stream.

He hadn't gone far when a sharp scent struck his nose. Granite stopped. The hair on his back stood high as he peered into the shadows, trying to locate the source. He saw nothing.

Carefully, he took a single step. Something hissed. The puppy's tail fell. He froze, trembling and afraid to move. He waited for a long time, his heart beating fast and a bad taste in his mouth. Then a ragged cloud blew past the moon and Granite saw a shaggy animal crouched beside a large rock. It was bigger than the puppy and its sharp teeth glistened in the dim light. Caught between its paws was a half-eaten snowshoe hare.

The wolverine snarled, warning the little dog to leave.

Wolverines are not wolves but enormous weasels. They have beautiful striped coats, blue eyes, short bushy tails, and long, sharp claws. They are mean fighters, but they are smaller than huskies and not as brave. Granite was too little to be dangerous, and the wolverine knew it.

The smell of fresh meat made the dog's mouth water, but he had no hope of tasting it. If he were lucky, he'd get away before the wolverine decided that puppy made a better meal than hare. Still frightened, the little dog pressed close to the ground, hunching his shoulders. He waited, not sure whether he should stay motionless or back slowly away.

After what seemed like a long time, the wolverine relaxed but its eyes glittered like diamonds. It hissed again and bared its teeth.

Slowly, Granite edged away from the stream, his tail dragging. As he moved back among the trees, he saw the wolverine take a large bite of hare.

It was clear that the forest was dangerous before

dawn. Granite remembered the night sounds he had heard from the kennel and searched for a hiding place. He found a mossy spot between the roots of a tall spruce and curled up to wait until full light.

Time passed slowly. He missed the warm bodies of his brothers and sister, and he missed the loving good-night licks of Seppala's tongue. Thinking about them made him feel so bad that he whimpered quietly. Finally, he slept.

A bird call woke him. The forest looked different with the sun streaming through the trees. Little moss flowers dotted the ground, and creamy dogwood blossoms nodded in the breeze. Here and there wild roses bloomed.

High above him, a gray jay settled softly on a spruce tip. It tilted its head to one side, then the other, and dropped to a lower branch. It hopped from one foot to the other.

The jay's company made Granite feel better. He knew it would squeal and fly away if danger threatened. His fear at rest, the puppy began grooming his legs. With his sharp teeth, he picked thorns and spruce needles out of his coat.

The jay fluttered to the ground and hopped around in a circle. It spied a bug crawling across a rose leaf and snapped it up.

As Granite watched, his stomach rumbled. Very slowly, he got to his feet and tensed his muscles. Just as he sprang, the jay flew up with a squawk and a great rustle of feathers. From the branch above Granite's head it screamed, insulting the puppy's hunting ability, his looks, and his pedigree.

The day had not started well. Granite sighed and returned to the stream, where he drank his fill. The morning sun warmed his back and dried his coat. Feeling better, he began to explore. He kept his nose to the ground, sniffing to see what animals had been there before him. Most of the smells were old. A bear had been through, but so long ago that the puppy had to sniff hard to catch its traces.

Soon Granite forgot his troubles. He chased a butterfly, rolled in a clump of wild celery, and chewed on a spruce cone. For a while, he ignored his empty stomach. Then a fresh scent reminded him how hungry he was.

It came from a clump of blueberry bushes, heavy with ripening fruit. The scent was strong. It was ground squirrel. The little dog's mouth began to water. The smell might be his dinner. Excited, he shoved his nose between the bushes. There, carefully hidden from passing animals, was the mouth of a burrow.

Granite dug hard. The dirt flew between his back feet and piled up in great dark heaps. He worked for a long time, longer than he had ever worked before. Worn out, he stopped to rest.

From the branch of a nearby tree he heard an angry chatter. He looked up, and far above him saw the squirrel, outlined against the sky. Its thin tail lay along the branch. Screaming "Sik! Sik!" the squirrel scolded the puppy for destroying its doorway. Then it whirled about, scampered down the trunk and up another tree. Granite watched as a branch bounced and swayed under the squirrel's weight. It ran along the limb and was gone.

Frustrated, Granite grabbed a nearby stick and dragged it around in circles. He shook it hard, pretending it was the squirrel, then tossed it to one side. The pretense made him feel a little better, but when it was over, he was still hungry.

All day Granite searched for food. He watched carefully for signs that might betray the passage of an unwary mouse beneath the carpet of spruce needles. Several times he saw the needles rustle and pounced, but with no success. The puppy was still so small that he landed short and his prey escaped.

Giving up on the idea of mouse, Granite looked

for berries. He ate a few buffalo berries, but the yellowish fruit was bitter. He had almost given up when he came upon a rotten log. Under the bark, he found a few fat beetles. He snatched one, but the others scurried away before he could grab them. He was still hungry.

The sun disappeared. Granite trotted through the shadows, searching for a safe place to spend the twilight hours. Suddenly a great gray owl swooped down, passing so close that the breeze from its deep wingbeats ruffled his fur. He scrambled under a buffalo berry bush, his heart beating against his ribs.

Without a sound, the owl settled on an overhanging branch. Peering through the branches, Granite could see its white throat and the shine of its large yellow eyes. The owl shifted from foot to foot, then hooted several times.

The fur rose on the back of Granite's neck. He made himself as small as possible. After a time, the owl silently flew off. Too frightened to think about food, Granite settled down to sleep. Putting his head between his front paws, he curled his tail over his nose. He listened to forest sounds until he fell asleep.

7. *Danger at Dusk*

Granite woke to sunlight. Through the spruce branches overhead, he saw blue sky and white clouds. The sun had slipped behind the mountains four times since he left the kennels.

During those days, he had eaten only insects, leaves, grass, a few green berries, and the growing tips of bushes. Hunger was always with him. To fill his stomach, he gulped water from the stream, but the cold water sometimes did not stay down. Often he thought sadly of kibble and meat—a great bowlful.

Granite knew he had to eat. He trotted through the trees, watching for signs of an unwary squirrel or a careless bird. He would have been happy with the smallest mouse, but no matter how hard he tried, he captured nothing.

The little dog's wanderings took him out of the

forest and up into the hills and along a river that wound between the mountains, its coils shining in the sun. His journey brought him to a valley, but he found no more food here than in the old land.

As Granite left the trees and moved into a meadow, a cloud of tiny flies whirled around him. His fur was so thick that they could not reach his skin, but they swarmed into his ears and eyes. He flicked his ears and shook his head, trying to chase them away. He fought the insects for several minutes, but nothing seemed to discourage them.

A sudden crack made him look up. What he saw swept all thoughts of insects out of his head.

In front of him, so close he could see their fur blowing in the breeze, stood a grizzly and her three cubs. Their backs were toward him. The bears were at the edge of the clearing, the mother feeding on a bed of lacy green plants while her cubs tore at nearby clumps of tall grass. As Granite watched, the mother moved to a patch of tall, flowering plants. When she settled down to eat, she was facing him.

Hoping she would not see him, Granite stopped. He stood so still that he did not even blink when insects flew into his eyes.

The mother bear's body was pale brown and her legs were dark. She was the biggest animal Granite had ever seen. She was bigger than Tim and Kate and the stranger put together. She had long claws and sharp teeth that could tear a puppy apart.

Every few minutes, the bear held her head high and tossed her muzzle about, checking for strange scents. She had not noticed Granite for the same reason that he had not noticed her. A crosswind carried their scents away.

One of the cubs tired of grubbing for grass. It cuffed another cub. The two little bears rolled on the ground, just as Digger and Granite often did. The third cub danced around them, waiting to wrestle the winner.

The mother raised her head. She growled softly.

The cubs ignored her. They tumbled over the ground, moving closer to Granite with each roll.

The mother bear got to her feet. She started toward the cubs, but she was not in a hurry.

Before she reached them, one of the pesky flies darted into Granite's nose. A terrible tickling sensation filled his head. He fought the feeling, but it was no use. He could not hold back the sneeze. It exploded with a roar that rolled across the clearing.

The mother bear stopped. She reared up on her hind legs and moved her head from side to side.

Her rounded ears stood erect and her small, black eyes blinked as she searched for the source of the sound. She found Granite and squinted, trying to decide what he was.

Granite waited, not daring to breathe.

The bear made a strange noise that sounded like "Huff! Huff!" She made it again.

The sounds were not loud. When the cubs heard the danger signal, they stopped playing and ran to her side.

Still Granite did not move. If he fled, the bear would surely charge. So he hunched down and tried to look like a rock. He hoped she would decide that a puppy was too small to bother about.

For a long time, the bear and the little dog stared at each other.

Then the bear raised her front paws and thumped the ground. She thumped the ground again. And again.

Granite didn't know whether she was warning him to leave or announcing a charge. He soon found out.

The bear gave a terrifying roar. Then she flattened her ears, lowered her head, and broke into a rocking run.

Granite's legs trembled, but he did not move.

The bear's powerful legs covered the ground with great bounds. As she ran toward the little dog, her head and massive shoulders looked as broad as Tim's truck. She came closer and he felt the heat of her breath. At the last minute, when he had given up all hope, the bear veered to one side and crashed past him.

Granite whirled around. Behind him, he saw a caribou calf running for cover.

Perhaps the bear saw the lone calf while she was charging. Perhaps it had been her target from the first. Granite had no way of knowing and didn't much care.

Without waiting to see if the calf escaped, he ran into the trees as fast as his short legs could carry him. He reached the stream and splashed into it. He drank thirstily, then trotted for a time in the shallow water.

After Granite left the stream, he looked for a place to rest. Not far from the water's edge, he found a log that had fallen against a large spruce. He squirmed under the log and curled up against the spruce trunk.

The space smelled of the squirrel that had used it before him. It also smelled of something else.

Granite caught the scent of food. He dug beneath the fallen log and unearthed a cache of seeds, which he ate greedily.

When he had swallowed the last seed, Granite thought about home. The picture of his mother's face filled his head, and he whimpered. He felt alone and sad. He was still sad when he fell asleep.

Granite slept for a long time. He slept the rest of the day and all that twilight. When he awoke, rays of sun streamed through the trees, making pools of light on the forest floor. He stretched and shook himself, then started a search for food.

Except for a few beetles and a cricket or two, he found nothing to eat that day. He was too discouraged to play and too clumsy to catch any mice or squirrels.

Before the shadows gathered, Granite reached the edge of the forest. Not far away, a rocky hillside rose toward the sky. Between the boulders were splashes of orange and yellow and pink and white flowers. He sat beneath a tree and studied the slope, hoping to spot a cave that would shelter him from bears.

It grew dim. The color faded from the hillside. The sky clouded over. Granite sniffed deeply, but found no danger in the air. Boldly, he trotted out of the trees. A strong wind blew from his back, bending the fireweed and ruffling his coat.

He had forgotten that it was impossible to smell animals downwind of him. He had also forgotten that the wind at his back carried his scent toward any animal in his path.

As he climbed the hill, picking his way among the rocks, a large body hurtled toward him. It passed so close that the odor of cat stung his nose. Startled, Granite slipped and tumbled down the rocks, rolling over and over to the foot of the hill. He landed in a heap, his front paw bent under him. He tried to stand, but his leg crumpled.

Back up the hill loomed a gray lynx, its yellow eyes glowing like twin fires. It gathered itself to leap. Just before it sprang, a long, low howl rang through the shadows. The lynx wheeled and fled in the opposite direction, bounding silently through the bushes.

Granite looked up to see a great black form standing on a high rock. It was a wolf.

8. The Kidnapping

About the time Granite tugged his first flake of hay across the grass, a white wolf moved her five pups from their rocky den to a high meadow bounded by a mountain stream. Under Snowdrift's watchful eye, the pups romped each day in the grass while the pack slept.

Late each afternoon, Ebony, the black wolf who was her mate, led the pack away, leaving Snowdrift to care for the pups. The adult wolves trotted in single file, with the yearling Climber following close to his father. Behind him came Ebony's brother Strider, Climber's older brother Roamer, and Breeze, a female who had come to them from a pack that hunted far to the west, past the place where the sun set.

After the pups got used to their new home, Snowdrift sometimes went off by herself to hunt, never traveling far. While she was gone, her pups wrestled, played "leap-wolf," and chased insects. When they tired, they lay on the grass and chewed on bones.

The pups were too small to hunt, but they were well fed. When the pack came back from a hunt, the pups swarmed around the big wolves, sniffing their mouths and nipping their muzzles. At this signal, the wolves disgorged food eaten on the hunt.

On the afternoon that humans invaded the meadow, the pups were alone. A chill wind brought a strange scent across the grass, but the little wolves were not afraid. They had no reason to connect the smell with danger.

The humans crept quietly to the edge of the clearing and crouched in the brush. For a long time they watched the playing pups. They had been searching for young wolves to raise in captivity and then breed with dogs. The market for wolf-dog hybrids was growing rapidly, and humans paid high prices for hybrid pups.

One of the humans turned to the other, nodded, and pulled out a pistol. Taking careful aim at a pup, he fired. As the tranquilizer dart struck the pup's flank, it yelped. A second yelp followed, then a third, a fourth, and a fifth. Within minutes, the pups lay unconscious in the grass.

When Snowdrift returned, her stomach bulging with chunks of marmot, the resting spot in the tall grass was empty. The pups were gone.

Anxiously, she ran back and forth through the grass, searching for their scent. She found the place where the humans had hidden and their bodies had crushed the grass. Their smell hung over the meadow. Growling softly, the white wolf put her nose to the ground and followed the trail along the stream.

Snowdrift followed the scent for miles, losing it where the humans crossed the stream, but picking it up again on the far side. She followed the trail to its end on the shore of a lake, where the kidnappers had stowed the wolf cubs into a plane and flown away.

In the gathering dusk, Snowdrift howled at the empty sky. She could not believe that her pups were gone forever. Perhaps they were back in the meadow.

She retraced her steps. As she neared the place where she had crossed the stream, her pace quickened. Splashing through the water, she searched the meadow once more, sniffing in every corner, behind every rock, and beneath every bush. The meadow was empty.

Fighting against fear, Snowdrift left the meadow. She ran hard toward the den where the pups had been born. Scurrying down the tunnel, she searched the deserted den, inspecting each crevice.

Snowdrift did not give up. Each day, while the other wolves rested, she searched for her children. Each evening, while the other wolves hunted, she continued her search among the cabins scattered through the valley.

Venturing so close to humans was not safe, but Snowdrift paid no attention to danger. She lived on scraps she found in piles of garbage and on mice and squirrels and marmots she found along her journeys. Again and again, Snowdrift returned to the old den, even though she knew in her heart the pups would not be there.

After several weeks, her conviction that she would find her cubs crumbled. When Snowdrift returned to the den that July day, the pack was resting nearby. They often slept close to the den, because they knew that Snowdrift's sorrow would bring her back to the place where her pups had come into the world.

On this afternoon, Snowdrift was weary from her

travels. After greeting Ebony, she curled up in the shade and fell into a deep sleep. The sun sank behind the mountains, and still she slept. Patiently, the pack waited.

When Snowdrift awoke in the twilight, the pack greeted her and the hunt began. The wolves circled the hill and started down toward the forest. Before they had gone far, a breeze brought the scent of lynx. Ebony threw back his head and howled, warning the big cat to leave.

9. *Encounter with Wolves*

Ebony was the first to spot the puppy at the foot of the hill. The big black wolf stared at the little dog. There was no welcome in the wolf's eyes. Granite shrank under the steady gaze. The wolf looked over his shoulder, then settled back on his haunches to wait. Granite did not move.

Pebbles rattled, then Climber, a smaller wolf whose light coat was streaked with black, appeared at the rocky crest. Granite found him less frightening than the first wolf, perhaps because the black fur encircling his eyes made him look almost like a husky. This young wolf sat beside Ebony and contemplated the lonely little dog. Neither made a sound.

Granite didn't know whether they intended to help him or eat him. He tried to look harmless.

A third wolf emerged. Then a fourth and a fifth.

They formed a line along the ridge. Soon a sixth wolf appeared. It was Snowdrift. She had a thick ruff around her face, but she was thin and haggard. Her skin hung loosely on her frame, and she moved slowly, almost sadly. She stared at the ground, but nothing caught her interest.

With an abrupt motion, the white wolf raised her head. She breathed deeply. Her ears pricked forward. Straining to see in the dusk, she peered down the slope. At last she made out the small form at the foot of the hill. Her yellow eyes, which had been dull, shone with interest.

The white wolf bounded swiftly down the dark hillside, skirting boulders and leaping over gullies. In an instant she was at Granite's side, sniffing him over from muzzle to tail.

The puppy trembled with fear and pain.

The white wolf nosed Granite's injured leg, testing the paw and foreleg.

When she shoved at the sore place, he yelped.

She licked away the blood that trickled from a deep cut, then looked up at the silent wolves, silhouetted against the night sky. Stretching her neck, she barked softly.

The white wolf trotted back up the hill, her head held high, her tail hanging easily in a loose curve.

Granite was helpless. He waited, wondering what would happen to him.

Snowdrift licked Ebony's muzzle, wagging her tail sideways. He averted his head, never taking an eye off the little dog. She grabbed his muzzle gently between her teeth, then dropped it.

They exchanged a long glance, then Ebony stood up. He turned away.

Snowdrift darted back down the hill.

Granite drew back his ears and lowered his tail.

The white wolf reached his side. She whined softly, then fastened her teeth carefully on the back of Granite's neck and lifted him off the ground. She carried him up the slope and deposited him gently on the ground before the other wolves.

They looked the puppy over carefully, sniffing every inch of his body. Granite locked his jaws together, determined not to whimper. His heart beat fast.

Most of the wolves regarded him with silence, but Strider, a white-chested, gray male almost as big as the black wolf, bared his teeth and growled.

Granite stared at the ground. If he met the eyes of this gray wolf, he would be in trouble.

Then Snowdrift snarled and stepped forward. Ebony moved at her side. Both wolves pulled up the corners of their mouths, showing their teeth. Their ears were erect, wrinkles creased their foreheads, and the fur across their shoulders stood high. Their tails were stiff.

Strider fell silent. He backed off, his ears drawn back against his head and his tail tucked between his legs.

Without another sound, Snowdrift scooped up Granite and trotted up the hill. The puppy dangled beneath her jaws, swaying with each step. He was almost too heavy for the wolf to carry, and his legs bumped on rocks in the path. As the wolf climbed, Granite watched the rest of the pack run through the brush until they disappeared in the night shadows.

Near the top, Snowdrift leaped onto a narrow ledge that made a path around the hill. She carried Granite along this ledge, then jumped over several rocks and darted into an opening just wide enough for her to pass through. She carried him down a tunnel and into a wide chamber, where she dropped him onto the smooth earth floor.

The den was cool and dry and smelled of wolf, but the smells were old. No one had slept here for weeks.

Snowdrift bathed the little dog with her tongue.

She cleaned away all traces of the storm and the wild dash through the woods and gave his sore leg special attention.

Under the touch of her tongue, Granite's fear melted. For the first time since he left home, he felt safe. His weary muscles relaxed. Despite his hunger, he was soon fast asleep.

When Granite awoke, the black wolf stood over him. In the dim light, the brown eyes seemed darker and larger than they had on the mountain.

A small ball of fear grew inside Granite. He cowered before Ebony, who stared at him but made no sound. In an attempt to please the big wolf, Granite stretched up and licked the corners of his mouth, as he had seen the white wolf do.

To his surprise, Ebony opened his jaws wide, squeaked, and brought up a great heap of meat. It made a warm, foamy pile on the floor. Granite fell on the food, eating hungrily in great gulps.

Ebony watched Granite eat, but there was no warmth in his eyes. He had fed the pup only to humor Snowdrift. When the food was gone, he turned and trotted back out of the tunnel.

10. The Hunting Lesson

Within a couple of days, Granite's leg had healed enough for him to put his weight on it without yelping. Snowdrift watched the puppy take several steps, then motioned with her head.

Granite did not understand. He stood silently with his head down, watching her.

Snowdrift whined and motioned again. When Granite did not move, she trotted in back of him. Nudging the puppy's bottom with her nose, she shoved him toward the entrance.

Surprised, Granite crept cautiously through the tunnel and emerged into the late afternoon sun. He stood before the mouth of the den, blinking at the light, and breathed in the wonderful smells of earth and plants and flowers.

He looked around. Steep, rock-ribbed mountains rose on all sides, their tops covered with snow.

Below the peaks, the slopes glowed with patches of yellow and blue. Farther down, the bright pink of fireweed spread over the ground, giving way to tall trees near the bottom. Beneath the den, at the base of the hill, stretched a meadow bordered by a swift running stream.

Before he could see more, Snowdrift shoved him again. Ignoring the yips of protest, she shoved Granite down the hill, through the brush, and across the meadow.

When the puppy reached the stream, she let him rest while she drank. Under her watchful eye, Granite lapped up water until he was no longer thirsty. Then Snowdrift left him on the bank and took several steps into the meadow. She stopped, looked at the puppy, and moved her head.

This time Granite knew what she meant. He scrambled to his feet and pranced after her. They walked upwind through deep grass. Snowdrift put each foot down carefully. As she walked, she stretched her neck high and sniffed deeply, making her nose wrinkle.

Despite his sore leg, it was hard for Granite to walk as slowly as Snowdrift. Determined to please the white wolf, he copied her every move. He sniffed hard, but did not know what he was searching for. The scents were all mixed up—flowers and grass and spruce and cottonwood and willow and birds and mice and even smells from the pack.

Snowdrift stopped. She stood silently for a moment, her head cocked to one side, then leaped. Between her paws was a mouse. She waited until Granite had seen the mouse, then she swallowed it. She ran her tongue along her lips and peered closely at the puppy. She motioned with her head.

She walked a few more steps, sniffed twice, and looked down at him. She took another step, sniffed again, and again looked at Granite.

At last he understood. Snowdrift was teaching him to catch mice. Granite remembered the mice he had tried to catch when he was so hungry. And how his every attempt had failed. He knew that he must watch Snowdrift closely so that he could begin to feed himself.

Compared with the scent of other animals, mouse smells are not strong. But after a while the different odors sorted themselves out, and Granite separated mouse from all the rest. When this happened, he yipped with excitement. At the sudden sound, Snowdrift gave him an affectionate nudge, warning him to be quiet.

The next time she caught the scent, she froze.

Still as stone, she watched the grass intently. The blades trembled, as if a breeze were passing over them. Snowdrift stood up on her hind legs and dropped heavily, keeping both her forelegs stiff and straight.

Beneath her paw was a mouse. She tossed it to Granite and he gulped it down in a single swallow. He was still hungry. It takes a lot of mice to fill the stomach of even a small dog.

Snowdrift let Granite try to catch the rest of his dinner. He walked beside her, but he was not as quiet as the big wolf. Once he stepped on a twig that snapped loudly in the silent meadow. Then he knocked a pebble aside and sent it rattling across the ground. At last he moved silently, but he had trouble finding the mouse she had scented.

When Granite finally spotted movement, his drop was off the mark. His small paws came down on nothing but grass, and the mouse scampered away to safety.

After Granite missed the third mouse, he grew tired. A large white moth fluttered past his nose. Away he ran, all thoughts of the hunt gone.

The moth danced in the evening sky just above his head, flitting from one flower to another. Granite snapped at it but missed. He chased it across the meadow, but it stayed just out of reach.

Snowdrift ran after him. When she reached the little dog's side, she bared her teeth. With a jerk of her head, she smacked him with the side of her muzzle. Her long tooth was hard, and the blow hurt.

Granite felt ashamed. He had failed at his first task. He hung his head. Snowdrift licked his nose and he felt better. He nibbled her paw with love, promising to pay attention.

Snowdrift resumed the hunting lesson. Granite forced himself to watch the grass closely. He tried hard. The first mouse he spotted got away, and so did the second and the third and the fourth. Then it happened! Granite stared at the rustling grass, gave a mighty leap, and landed heavily on the mouse.

He caught only one more mouse that evening, but he could tell that Snowdrift was pleased. When the sky grew light and Granite curled up to sleep, his hunger was gone and he was filled with pride.

11. Dismal Days

The sun was high in the sky when Granite awoke to the cry of a wolf. From the other side of the stream, a howl rose, wavered, and dropped. The sound brought Snowdrift to her feet. She threw back her head and howled in reply, then splashed through the water and scrambled up the far bank.

Through the trees came Ebony, followed by the rest of the pack. In his mouth, the leader held a haunch of caribou.

Snowdrift bounded up to him, her tail wagging rapidly and her body wriggling with joy. She licked Ebony's muzzle. He pranced in front of her, turning his head so that she could see the great piece of meat he carried.

The pack crossed the creek and entered the meadow. Ebony dropped the caribou before Snowdrift and stepped back. The white wolf fell on the meat, tearing off large pieces and swallowing them.

At the sight of food, water filled Granite's mouth. He was suddenly hungry. He scampered to Snowdrift's side, ready to eat.

Before Granite could snatch a morsel, Snowdrift growled. She snapped fiercely, her teeth closing in the air close to the puppy's head.

Granite cringed, terrified at the sudden change in her behavior. Until now, Snowdrift had been kind and loving. Now she would not let him eat. Backing away, he lay down several feet from the meat and watched.

Breeze, her stomach swollen with meat she had eaten at the kill, walked to Granite's side. She favored her left hind foot, which was missing two pads. She was a gray wolf with a yellowish face. When she looked down at the puppy, her wide-spaced, yellow eyes were cold. She did not care for this orphan that Snowdrift had adopted, but she obeyed the pack leaders' decisions.

Granite got up, whined, and wagged his tail. When Breeze did not growl, he licked the side of her mouth. She motioned and stepped away. Granite followed, jumping up and nipping at her muzzle with every step.

Just as Ebony had done in the den, Breeze

opened her jaws wide enough to engulf the little dog's head, then squeaked. A cascade of warm meat hit the grass in front of him. He gulped the chunks of caribou, his eyes fixed fearfully on the other wolves.

Before Granite could finish, Strider ran up, grabbed the biggest piece of caribou, and darted off. Breeze saw him take the meat but did nothing. Her job was to provide Granite with food, not to make sure that he ate it.

When Snowdrift had finished her meal, there were only a few shreds of flesh left on the bone. She walked to the place where the pack rested and lay down.

Climber looked around warily, then hurried to the bone. He grabbed it and carried it away. Far from the drowsy pack, he settled down to chew on his prize.

With his stomach full, Granite walked slowly to Snowdrift's side. He curled up beside her but was careful not to touch her. This time he did not relax and go to sleep. Instead, he watched Snowdrift, hoping for some signal. He was confused and ready to flee at the faintest growl.

To his surprise, she whined a welcome and began to bathe him. As the wolf licked his face and belly,

Granite pondered the sudden changes in her behavior. He did not know that he had broken an important rule of the pack when he tried to eat before one of the pack leaders had finished her meal. Nor did he know that Breeze had fed him only because Ebony insisted on it.

Through the long summer, Snowdrift treated Granite like her own pup. It may have been his blue eyes that made her so loving. Baby wolves have blue eyes, but they soon change color, turning yellow or brown. Granite's eyes were always the color of a summer sky.

Snowdrift let Granite pull her tail, tackle her, and leap over her sleeping body. When she wearied of his attention, she pinned the puppy to the ground and, with a gentle growl, let him know that she wanted to sleep.

Although Ebony had no interest in Granite, he protected him because Snowdrift had taken the pup as her child. He made the other wolves feed the little dog, even when there was not enough to satisfy their own hunger.

The wolves resented the task, but they obeyed Ebony. They carried back food from the hunt, sometimes in their stomachs and sometimes in their jaws. Often they brought Arctic hare, which was easy to catch because its white fur stood out against the brush. They brought snowshoe hare, whose gray summer coat made it harder to catch. They brought sheep and they brought caribou. When they could find nothing else, they brought ground squirrel.

Although the wolves fed Granite, he could tell that they did not like him. If Snowdrift was not watching, they often snatched back the food they brought. Sometimes they stole so much of the puppy's food that he went hungry.

Granite's only playmate was Climber, who had been a puppy the year before. Perhaps the pair got along so well because the black markings on Climber's face reminded Granite of his mother and brothers. Perhaps they got along because Climber was too young to hate the dog.

All the wolves liked Climber. The long guard hairs over his shoulders stuck out in every direction, making him look always ready for a game. He played pranks on the big wolves. Sometimes he pounced on them while they slept. Sometimes he jumped in front of them from behind a rock or bush along the trail. When he did this, the wolves wagged their tails and nuzzled him. Granite soon learned that the other wolves would not tolerate such behavior from him. When he tried to join in the play, they snarled at him.

Climber seemed to forget that Granite was only a dog. During the long afternoons, the pair had great games of tag, tussled over bones, and ran after birds and butterflies.

Granite found it fun, except when Climber decided to practice his fighting skills. Then he leaped on the puppy, bowled him over, and nipped him until he yelped. When Climber did this, Granite thought of Digger.

The days passed, but Granite still missed his family. When he curled up to sleep, their pictures danced in his head. Each time he woke up whimpering with homesickness, Snowdrift licked his face and quieted his cries.

Sometimes life in the pack was painful. Ebony and Breeze simply pretended that Granite did not exist between feedings, but Strider and Roamer did everything they could to make the little dog's life miserable. When he came near them, they growled. When he was slow to move away, they cuffed him with a heavy paw. When they saw him chewing on a bone, they took it away—even though they did not want it for themselves.

Granite did not know why they hated him. Later

he understood that Strider wanted no outsiders in the pack, especially dogs. He thought they were weak animals, whose short legs could never keep up the hunting pace set by the wolves. If Strider had been pack leader, Granite knew he would have died on the night they found him.

Roamer worshipped Strider and copied the gray wolf's every act. Roamer was a year older than Climber and considered himself an adult. His coat was black, except for a yellowish streak behind each shoulder and a scattering of silver hairs along his sides. He hated Granite because Strider did.

Most of the time, Granite managed to stay out of their reach. He learned to keep several wolves between him and his persecutors while he drank. He learned to stop his play and walk off when games with Climber took him near the sleeping males. He learned to stay at Snowdrift's side when Strider and Roamer were awake and moving about the meadow. But even with the white wolf to protect him, a glance from Strider sent a shiver of fear from Granite's nose to the tip of his tail. And the frosty glare in Roamer's eyes could stop him in mid-jump and send him hunting for Snowdrift.

12. The Rules of the Pack

During the summer, the pack moved from one meadow to another, following the caribou. Through those endless days, Snowdrift grieved for her lost pups. Her skin no longer hung loosely and her movements were quick, but the pain never left her eyes. Despite her love for Granite, she could not forget her lost children.

Since Granite first looked on the world, four moons had come and gone. His legs had grown and his strength increased. He could run a long time without tiring, farther and faster than on that day when he fled from the bearded stranger.

Now that Granite was older, the wolves insisted that he follow the rules of the pack. He tried, but at first his tail kept him in continual trouble. Wolves carry their tails hanging loosely, but like all Siberian huskies, Granite carried his tail high. It was white and thick and beginning to curl over his back. To the rest of the pack, it was a flag of defiance.

Each time Granite passed near another pack member, his lofty tail provoked snarls and nips. Breeze, who mostly ignored him, could not overlook a waving tail, and sometimes it was too much for Snowdrift.

At first Granite did not know that the position of a tail sent a message to the pack. Wolves' tails stand tall only when they catch the scent of prey or feel especially good about themselves. The pup's bushy tail told the wolves that he was an impudent youngster who did not accept the law of the pack.

As Granite watched the wolves carefully, he learned that the tail was the wolf's badge of rank. Ebony held his own tail high. When the leader walked by other wolves, their tails drooped and they lowered their heads. Even Snowdrift, who was almost as powerful within the pack as Ebony, sometimes did this.

Then he noticed that Climber cringed before Roamer just as all the wolves cringed before Ebony and Snowdrift. In the same way, Roamer was careful to keep his tail down when Strider was near.

It was weeks before Granite could keep his own

tail down without effort. Even then, he sometimes forgot. When this happened, a snarl soon reminded him to drop the offending tail.

Before he arrived, Climber was the lowest male in the pack. Now that position belonged to Granite. Climber was friendly, but pleased to have someone beneath him. He watched Granite's tail as closely as did Strider, but as soon as it drooped, he forgot the offense and was ready to play.

One afternoon in late summer, the pack slept sprawled in the shade. The cottonwoods had begun to turn the slopes yellow, but the air was hot and still. No leaf turned. Searching for the slightest whisper of wind, Granite stretched out on his stomach, with his nose on his paws.

A sharp nudge from Climber woke the sleeping dog. In his mouth, Climber held a piece of sheepskin, the remains of an old kill. He shook it, backed up a few steps, then shook it again.

It was an invitation to play. Granite's eyes brightened. Despite the heat, he jumped up, grabbed one end of the hide, and began to pull. As the pair tugged the hide back and forth, the game took them away from the slumbering pack and out into the sunny meadow.

With a sudden jerk, Climber tore the sheepskin

free and ran several steps through the grass. Before Granite could follow, a sudden shadow fell over the meadow. Granite looked up to see an enormous eagle diving toward Climber.

The hide fell from Climber's mouth. The eagle swooped low, screamed "Kyaa!" and swerved up again, just in time to escape Climber's snapping jaws.

As the bird rose in the air, Granite saw a wash of golden feathers across the back of its dark head. With wings spread wide, the eagle seemed as big as Ebony.

The eagle turned and swooped again. Again Climber leaped into the air and snapped.

The cruel hook of the eagle's beak and the spread of its curved talons made Granite think that the bird was attacking Climber. Fear rose in the dog's throat, and kept him from going to the young wolf's aid. Once more the eagle dived toward Climber. This time, Granite's feeling for his friend outweighed his fear. His muscles tensed, but before he could move, he realized that the dives were a game—at least for the eagle.

After the bird had swooped down more times than there were wolves in the pack, Climber became annoyed. He barked.

At the sharp sounds of distress, the resting wolves awoke. Roamer raised his head, stretched, and trotted to Climber's rescue. On the eagle's next pass, he leaped beside his brother. Teeth clicked in the air, and a single feather floated to the ground.

The eagle was not ready to flirt with the jaws of two wolves. With the game over, it flew away. Through the empty air drifted a final "Kyaa!"

Roamer picked his way back to the pack, walking carefully, his head held high. He passed Granite without a glance, but a low growl drifted back on the still air.

As the sun sank toward the mountains, the pack got up. One by one, they stretched and began to play. Nipping Snowdrift's tail, Ebony began a game of tag. She chased him, with Breeze and Roamer close on her heels. It looked like so much fun that Granite scampered after them, but was left behind.

Panting, he watched Climber start a mock battle with Strider. The young wolf rushed at Strider, shoved the older wolf with a shoulder and dashed away. Strider chased Climber, nudged the youngster, and stood up, throwing his front legs over Climber's shoulder. Back and forth they ran, leaping and tumbling in the grass. It looked like a real fight, but their wagging tails said it was only a game.

Granite's excitement overcame his judgment. As Ebony ran past, the dog joined in, darting among legs and nipping at tails. For a time, no one paid attention. Then Strider noticed him. He snarled and lunged. With a swipe, he flipped Granite over.

The dog tumbled across the grass, coming to rest at the base of a small rock. He scrambled to his feet, but did not plunge back into the playing pack. He was afraid of Strider's teeth and paws.

The romp ended when Ebony threw back his head and howled. At once the other wolves rushed over and formed a circle, almost touching. Together they sang, their muzzles pointing at the sky, their eyes bright and their tails wagging. The music rang through the air and into the corners of the valley. The wolves sang of the joy of the hunt and their trust in the pack.

Granite was too small to join the circle, but he sang anyway. It was a happy time.

When the song was finished, Ebony started off at an easy lope, his tail swinging and his head high. The rest of the pack followed him in single file—all but Snowdrift. With Granite, she watched the hunters ford the stream and disappear among the tall cottonwoods.

As the early light shone through leaves that shivered gold in the morning breeze, the first hunter returned. Long before the wolf could be seen, his howls alerted Snowdrift and Granite.

It was Ebony. He was alone, and he brought no meat. Snowdrift greeted him with happy whines and high-pitched squeals. She licked his face. He whined in reply and called for the pair to follow him.

Granite did not know where Ebony was taking them. At Snowdrift's side, he splashed through the water and ran after the pack leader. Ebony loped along a well-marked path that wound through trees, between low hills, and up a slope scattered with blueberry, cranberry, and rhododendrons.

Snowdrift and Granite followed Ebony over a rise. Before they saw the pack below them, they heard the raucous cries of ravens perched in trees above the fallen caribou. The two wolves and the dog ran down the slope toward the pack. It was the first time Granite had been taken to a kill site. He felt grown up.

As they neared the feeding wolves, Strider saw them. To Granite's surprise, he stopped eating and drew back. So did the other wolves.

Ebony and Snowdrift stepped up and began to eat. Though Granite was hungry, he did not join them. He had learned his lesson well.

The leaders ignored the noisy ravens, who fluttered above them, swooping down at times to snatch a mouthful of meat. While Ebony and Snowdrift fed, the rest of the pack danced around them, whining. The pair paid no attention. They ate and ate until Granite thought they would eat everything, even the bones.

At last they finished. Hoping for a signal to eat, the rest of the pack crawled toward the kill. They moved on their bellies, their tails curled tightly between their legs.

Ebony did not allow the other wolves to feed at once. Instead, he stood over the kill and snapped at each wolf who came too close. Only after they pled with him and licked his muzzle did he let them eat.

The pack rushed to the meal, but Granite did not follow them. He waited until Roamer and Strider had torn off several chunks of meat. When he thought they were absorbed in their food, he rushed in, hoping to snatch a bite.

Strider saw the little dog. He snarled and snapped, his teeth closing in the air near Granite's head. The dog fell back. After a time, he took a cautious step toward the kill. Again Strider snarled a warning.

Afraid to make another try, Granite waited while

Strider ate. He ate for a long time. When he finished, he raised his head and glared at Granite. Then he walked away. A black cloud of ravens flew down and began to eat.

Still Granite waited. He waited until Strider lay down beside Breeze. He waited even longer. He waited until Roamer was sprawled out asleep. Only then did Granite dare to take a mouthful.

13. A Cruel Trick

A night wind came up, pushing streamers of black clouds across the moon. With a mournful cry, an owl flew low over the grass, searching for its dinner. On this night, the pack did not hunt.

The last kill had given the wolves more meat than they could eat. Through the autumn afternoons and into the evenings, the pack slept near the food cache. They would not leave until only bones and hair were left.

With no need to hunt, the wolves were free to do whatever they liked. After playing with the pack, Snowdrift and Ebony wandered into the dark forest, happy to be alone. Breeze took Roamer and Climber along a rocky ridge to practice their hunting skills. Left without a playmate, Granite chased after moths and sniffed out mice.

A soft bark pulled him away from his games.

Strider stood at the edge of the clearing. He motioned for Granite to follow him. He had never done this before.

Fearfully, Granite trotted over to where the gray wolf stood. The dog was careful to keep his tail hanging down and his nose close to the ground. Standing silently, Strider stared at him. As quickly as he could, Granite rolled onto his back and slowly wagged his tail from side to side.

Granite's submission seemed to satisfy Strider. Again he motioned with his head, then turned and set off on a path that led to the lake.

Keeping a safe distance behind, Granite followed the big gray wolf. The fear that had fluttered through the little dog at the sound of the wolf's bark faded. Perhaps Strider had decided to accept him as a pack member. A good feeling began to grow inside Granite. He tried to look as alert and confident as a hunter.

The pair traveled for some time. Once Granite heard mice rustling in the grass. Strider trotted on. Granite smelled ground squirrel. Strider paid no attention. An arctic hare, its white coat glimmering in the dark, bounded across the trail, then froze when it caught the scent of wolf. Strider loped by as if it did not exist.

Granite wondered what Strider was looking for. When they reached the lake, the wolf ran along the shore. He passed a group of nesting ducks without pausing, then turned toward the trees. His speed increased.

Suddenly he stopped and signaled for silence. Granite heard a series of grunts, then a low "coo-coo-coo." The dog's head filled with a strong scent of rotting wood.

As Granite stood quietly, he made out the form of a small animal. This strange-smelling creature reached no higher than the little dog's belly. It was chewing on a young spruce. After each mouthful, it stopped, held its head high, and sniffed the air. It was checking for danger. The creature felt safe because the wind blew toward the invaders, hiding their presence.

The moon rose out of the clouds. Its light glinted on the silver tips of the creature's bulky coat and on the long, curved teeth that stripped away at the tender growth. With its small paws, it grasped the sapling just as humans hold things in their hands. Granite had never seen such an odd-looking creature.

Strider motioned toward it.

Granite's excitement grew. Strider was giving

him a hunting lesson. The dog looked at the wolf, wanting to be sure that Strider had given permission to hunt.

Again he motioned toward the creature.

Granite felt grown up. He was determined to show Strider that he could hunt as well as a wolf.

Granite crept close, making no sound. He hoped that Strider noticed that he was careful to stay in back of the creature, where it could neither see nor smell the approaching dog. Granite stopped. He tensed his muscles. When his prey bent its head for another bite, Granite sprang.

In two bounds, the dog reached his target. He opened his jaws. Granite was about to close his teeth on a meal when he heard a chattering sound. Something smacked the dog's neck. Hard.

Howling, Granite pulled back. He was on fire with countless points of pain. His throat and leg bristled with porcupine needles.

Strider shook his head with disdain. He moved forward and circled the porcupine. Jerking its tail from side to side, the porcupine turned with him. It tried to keep its tail toward the wolf, but Strider was faster. After several circles in one direction, Strider reversed himself and ran the other way. The porcupine did the same.

After several more circles, the porcupine wavered. It seemed dizzy. At once, Strider darted in, grabbed the porcupine by the nose, and flipped it over on its back.

He had given Granite a hunting lesson, and one that the young dog would not soon forget. Strider knew that Granite had never before seen a porcupine. He knew that the dog would attack it from the rear. And he knew that the porcupine would defend itself with its quill-laden tail. Granite's lesson had been a cruel one.

Strider did not offer the little dog any food. While the wolf filled his stomach with porcupine, Granite used his teeth to pull the sharp quills from his front leg. Each time he yanked a quill free, the barbs cut his flesh and blood ran down his paw.

When Strider had finished his meal, he walked over to where the pup lay, whimpering. Granite's leg still throbbed and his throat burned.

Strider brought his face close to the dog's. The wolf's brown eyes glowed, and the light glistened on his fangs.

Granite closed his eyes tight. A small ball of fear in his stomach threatened to explode. There was a stab of pain. Granite opened his eyes.

Strider's nose had nudged a quill embedded in

Granite's leg. The wolf was peering at Granite, taking careful note of the damage. He sniffed the scent of Granite's blood. When he was satisfied, he stepped away. His cold gaze drilled into Granite's blue eyes. The young dog pulled back. Without making a sound, he let Granite know that he was an incompetent hunter and always would be one. Granite understood that Strider would never allow him to be part of the pack.

14. The First Hunt

The meadow glittered in the morning sun. Granite's paws melted the thin covering of frost and left a dark trail across the silvery grass. For a long time, he and Climber dashed back and forth, making intricate patterns.

A flock of black-necked, gray geese flew over the lake, their wings beating against the wind. They honked loudly, turned, and came back. Granite watched them land far out on the water, their great wings extended and their feet stretched out in front of them, sending up a spray as they glided across the surface.

His attention caught by their honking, Climber also turned toward the water. Near the shore, swam a flock of golden-eyed ducks. The ducks were feeding, and the playing pair watched them disappear under the water and pop to the surface.

Climber was ready for another game. He lay flat on his stomach and edged toward the water.

They had played this game before. Granite flattened himself and scooted on his stomach beside Climber. The ducks did not see them.

They moved slowly, making no sound. When they were close to the lake, Climber looked at Granite. The dog returned his glance. He nodded.

Together, they burst to their feet and charged the ducks. As the pair reached the water's edge, the flock exploded, taking wing as the wolf and dog splashed into their midst. Climber's eyes glowed with happiness and his tongue lolled out of his mouth. They splashed in the shallow water for a time, then bounded onto the bank. Together, they shook themselves, sending showers of water.

The fall colors soon faded, and the mountain peaks turned white with snow. The ducks and geese had flown south. The wolves had to break through ice to drink from the streams. The days were short, and stars spread across the sky before the pack trotted off on the hunt.

Granite always felt bad when the pack left. He watched the hunters sadly as they traveled down the trail. His eyes followed Ebony, who never noticed the dog. Except at playtime, the leader moved proudly among the pack, his body erect as he accepted the respect of the other wolves. Only Snowdrift did not cringe before him. He was stern, but never cruel, and he was a magnificent hunter.

Granite longed to be like him and ached to hunt at his side. But Ebony judged the young dog too careless to run with the hunters.

While the pack was gone, Granite practiced hunting mice. Each evening he did this, bounding through the fireweed and scattering the feathery seeds like drifting snowflakes. Soon he was catching a mouse on almost every pounce.

Granite shared his prey with Snowdrift. Ebony must have found out, because one evening it happened.

Ebony howled for the pack to gather. The wolves stopped their play and joined him in the clearing beside the lake. But he did not begin the song of the hunt. Instead he waited quietly, his eyes on Granite.

Granite wondered if he had done something wrong. He pretended to search for a flea, nibbling along his leg. When the dog looked up, Ebony was still watching him.

Granite huddled on the ground, his ears back and tail between his legs. He had no idea what rule of the pack he had broken, but he expected to find out. Granite waited for Snowdrift to show him how to placate Ebony.

At last the pack leader barked and motioned for the dog to join the rest of the wolves.

Granite could not believe it. He scrambled to his feet and ran over to the pack, his legs moving so fast that he skidded into Strider when he tried to stop. The gray wolf smacked the dog with his paw, but Granite didn't care. He was going on the hunt.

As the pack raised their voices in the hunting song, Granite howled as loudly as he could. The sounds soared, wavered, and soared again, weaving a wonderful melody.

The last notes of the song trailed away on the wind. Ebony trotted off along the side of the lake. Snowdrift was next, with Granite close behind. The dog's heart swelled with pride. The rest of the pack followed.

A full moon rode high in the sky, casting shadows across the trail. The wolves traveled for a long time, looking for sheep or caribou. Granite grew weary, wondering if they would run all night and come home with empty stomachs.

Suddenly Ebony stopped. He turned and sniffed deeply. His tail rose into the air. The rest of the pack lifted their heads, drawing in the air noisily. Granite sniffed, too. The wind carried the smell of moose.

Without a word, the pack gathered in a circle, nose to nose. Granite stood between Snowdrift and Climber.

The strong smell told the wolves that a cow moose and her calf were close. The wind blew against the pack, keeping their scent from the prey.

Granite yipped softly with excitement.

Ebony batted him, but gently. The leader knew the thrill of a first hunt, and Granite's cry was so faint that it had not alarmed the moose. He motioned for the dog to stay behind the other wolves, where he would not be in danger.

Strider moved in behind Ebony and Snowdrift. Granite fell back, trotting between Roamer and Climber. The wolves loped easily in the direction of the scent, still strung out in a line. Every wolf peered ahead, tails wagging, eager to sight the prey.

On the other side of a clump of trees, Ebony picked up the trail. The smell of moose grew stronger, rising from each hoofprint in the soft earth.

Ebony ran faster. They covered the ground quickly, with rising excitement. They were on a steep slope, covered with boulders and bushes. When they reached the crest, the wolves could see the moose and her calf below, lying in a willow thicket.

They ran down toward the moose. Granite was careful not to step on any branches or dislodge any stones. The wind still blew toward the pack, so the moose could not smell them.

The wolves were only ten moose lengths from the sleeping pair when the cow raised her head and saw them. She scrambled to her feet and herded her calf out into a frosty meadow that glittered in the moonlight.

The pack fanned out. Granite watched carefully. When the wolves stopped moving and crouched, he did the same. The wolves' eyes were fixed on the moose, who stood motionless in the middle of the meadow.

The moose bolted for the trees, and the pack ran after them. After every step, the cow looked back at the pursuing pack.

The pack caught up with the cow, who slowed and stopped. She wheeled and planted her feet firmly, facing the wolves. Her hackles were raised and her eyes flamed red. The calf ran a few steps toward the distant trees, then checked his stride, waiting for his mother.

The cow swung her long neck at Ebony and lashed out at him with her forefeet. He twisted away. Again the moose struck at him. Eluding the slashing hooves, Ebony tried to run around the cow and reach the running calf. The cow turned, keeping herself between Ebony and the calf.

One after another, the big wolves tried to separate the calf from its mother. But she stayed in front of the calf, fending off the pack.

Before long Ebony had enough. He signaled, and the pack left the moose. Exhausted, they lay down where they were. Panting heavily, they watched the cow gather her calf and move toward the trees.

After a short rest, Ebony led the wolves across the meadow and up the next hill. They ran along the crest until he spotted a lone caribou grazing upwind. Within a few minutes, he and Snowdrift had brought it down.

There was enough meat for everyone. With full stomachs, the pack lay down to sleep.

15. Still a Clumsy Dog

Snow fell softly as the pack trotted down the trail. Granite, who was running just behind Snowdrift, opened his mouth wide to catch the big, fluffy flakes. They felt cool, but turned to water as soon as they touched his tongue. It was the first snow of the year. The deep cold was more than a month away.

Clouds covered the night sky, but the air was still. The flakes sifted straight down, sticking on branches and spruce needles.

The wolves had been running since the light faded and it was now nearly dawn. This was an important hunt. They had caught nothing for weeks. Until the fall colors vanished, hunting had been good. The wolves had eaten well.

Once three caribou fell in a single night, and the pack stayed near the kill for many days. After eating their fill, the wolves scraped earth and leaves over the meat. After that, they rested nearby, eating whenever they were hungry until there was not a scrap of meat on the bones.

Now their luck had changed. They found no sheep, and the caribou and moose either outran the pack or stood their ground.

As the days passed, Granite learned how hard it was to bring down a healthy animal. Only the old, the sick or injured, or calves that were separated from their mothers, fell to the wolves. Ten animals escaped for every one they caught. Sometimes the wolves lived for days on mice or squirrels, their stomachs always half empty.

On this night Granite began to tire. He lagged farther and farther behind Ebony and Snowdrift.

Again and again Strider nudged the dog's bottom, angry because he was holding up the hunt. Finally, the gray wolf snarled and snapped.

Ebony heard the commotion. He stopped abruptly and turned back. The pack formed a circle, noses pointing in.

Ebony crossed the circle and looked closely at Granite, his head turned to one side.

The dog pulled his tail between his legs and put back his ears. Fearful, he waited.

At last Ebony acted. He seemed to understand

the young dog's weariness and the gray wolf's part in the disturbance. Instead of snarling at Granite, he growled briefly at Strider, sending the gray wolf's tail down. Strider glared at the dog, but did nothing.

Ebony swung around and began to run, this time at a slower pace. Tired as Granite was, he managed to keep up with the pack. He did not want to disappoint Ebony.

The sky turned gray before Ebony left the trail and trotted up the hill to a safe resting place among the rocks. The wolves bedded down in the snow, turning around several times to hollow out beds. Curling their tails over their noses, they went to sleep hungry.

It was late afternoon when Granite opened his eyes. He shook himself, sending snow flying in all directions.

At first he thought he was alone, for he saw nothing but a broad expanse of snow. Yet he could smell the wolves. Then Granite noticed that he was surrounded by mounds of snow. From each mound rose cloud puffs of breath.

Granite stood up and stretched. The movements woke Climber, who lifted his head and looked first to the right, then to the left. Snow was heaped on his head, and he seemed to be showing off. Climber was ready for a frolic.

As soon as Granite gave the play sign, stretching out his front legs and raising his hindquarters, Climber got up. Shaking off snow, he bounded over.

The dog and the wolf romped through the snow, then thrust their noses deep into it. They stretched their necks and slid first their heads, then their entire bodies through the delicious cold. Granite thought it felt wonderful.

For a time, Breeze watched the pair play. To Granite's surprise, she joined them, her tail wagging. On her belly, she scooted into the fresh snow, twisting back and forth. Suddenly she stopped, raised her head high and sniffed the breeze. With a howl that echoed in the still air, she woke the other wolves.

Wondering what had excited her, Granite breathed deeply and caught the scent of distant sheep.

The pack was soon on the trail. They were still running when the sun sank below the mountains. In the twilight they came upon many sheep spread along an exposed ridge. The animals were grazing among dry grasses uncovered by the wind.

When Granite saw curled horns on every head, his heart sank. There were no calves here. The pack had found a herd of rams, and healthy rams have no trouble escaping a wolf pack. The wolves probably would not eat this night.

The pack settled down to watch the herd. The rams had their backs to the wolves. Since Dall sheep depend on sight to detect predators, they had not discovered their danger.

For some time, the wolves watched the herd from a distance. Then Granite learned the virtue of patience. First Ebony, then the rest of the pack, noticed that one of the rams had an injured leg. He could not run.

At Ebony's signal, the pack charged. Before the sheep knew that the wolves were among them, the lame ram was separated from the herd. The big wolves soon brought it down, ignoring the other sheep who ran up a nearby slope and escaped into the rocks.

Climber tried to help the hunters, but he got in Strider's way, making the gray wolf break step and fall behind the rest of the pack. Strider snapped at Climber, and the young wolf fell back beside Granite. Climber's hunting skills were not much better than those of the young dog, and that made the wolf unhappy. He wanted Ebony to be proud of him. Granite knew how Climber felt. The young dog wanted Ebony to be proud of him, too.

With their hunger satisfied for the first time in several weeks, the pack slept heavily for the rest of the night and through the following morning.

They were on the trail the next evening when Strider began tormenting Granite. He was loping just behind the dog. From time to time, he overran Granite and, using his shoulder, shoved the young dog heavily to one side. This threw Granite into the deep snow.

Each time Strider pushed him out of line, Granite floundered and had to work hard to get back to his place. When running in the snow, a pack travels fast because each wolf places its feet in the tracks of the wolf ahead. With the packed snow beneath their feet, wolves can move rapidly. After they go by, it looks as if only a single animal passed over the trail.

It was not long before the racket caught Ebony's attention. This time Strider's tricks worked. Ebony snarled at Granite and sent him back in the line. As Granite passed Roamer, the black wolf snapped at him. When the hunt resumed, Granite ran behind Climber, at the end of the line.

Before dawn the pack found a band of bull caribou, their dark brown coats standing out against the snow. As the wolves neared, the bulls turned to face them, lowering their great heads and showing their silvery manes and white antlers. Ebony took the pack past the caribou, making no attempt to attack.

The sky lightened, and Ebony searched for a rocky promontory where the wolves could sleep. As they were scratching out comfortable beds, a movement down the slope caught Granite's eye.

Below them, half hidden by a bush, a red fox feasted on frozen blueberries. Although the wind blew the wolves' scent toward the fox, it did not pause in its meal. The fox seemed not to care that a pack of hungry wolves was nearby.

Hoping to show Ebony how well he could hunt, Granite charged the fox. Before the dog had taken more than a dozen strides, a heavy shoulder jolted him off his feet. Granite tumbled over and over, gathering snow on his coat. As he started to get up, he was cracked by the side of a wolf's head.

Granite supposed that he was once again the victim of Strider's malice, but when the dog raised his head, he looked into the fierce yellow eyes of Breeze.

Granite cringed and pulled his tail between his legs. With head down and ears flattened against his head, the dog waited for another blow.

Nothing happened. Breeze stood over Granite, panting.

The dog waited, afraid to rise.

Breeze stepped back. She looked down the slope, then back at Granite. She did this several times, but the dog did not respond. Turning away, she took several careful steps down the slope. Then she walked warily in a wide circle, pausing and sniffing deeply before each step.

Satisfied, she edged in and began to dig. She dug cautiously, carving a cavity in the snow. When she was finished, she pulled away and again stared at Granite.

Granite saw only snow. He made no sign.

Breeze looked around. Her eye fell on a stick that had been uncovered when she dug. Grasping one end in her teeth, she edged toward the hole. She stretched out her neck and stabbed the stick into the snow.

A sharp snap split the silent air. Breeze dug again, this time rapidly. Soon a steel trap lay on the snow, its wicked jaws clamped tight on the stick.

Breeze walked up to Granite. She turned to one

side and thrust her back foot toward him. She looked toward the trap and wuffed twice. Then she looked back at him, her head tilted to one side.

At last Granite understood. Breeze had saved him from disaster. Having lost her footpads to one steel trap, she kept close watch for others.

Granite lifted his head and licked Breeze's face. She wagged her tail, nodded, and went back up the hill.

When the dog rejoined the pack, he sensed their disapproval. Ebony's eyes were stern and reproachful. His gaze made Granite feel like a tiny puppy. Climber looked the other way. Even Snowdrift was unhappy.

Strider growled. He showed his disgust by moving away and hollowing out a new bed as far from the pack as possible. Granite wondered if Strider was as disgusted with Breeze for warning him as with the dog's carelessness. Surely, if Strider had seen him running toward a trap, he would have let the dog blunder into it.

Granite went to sleep with a heavy heart. He had tried to show Ebony that he was worthy of the pack. Instead he had shown that he was a clumsy pup. Granite wondered if he would ever please his admired leader.

16. *Tragedy*

It was a time of endless night. Only a thin sliver of moon hung overhead, and the black sky burned with the cold fire of stars. The wolves ran along a packed drift at the base of the mountain, avoiding the trail, where the snow was soft.

Beneath the white blanket, ground squirrels and marmots slept snug in their burrows. The moon had come and gone several times since the bears disappeared into their dens.

Granite ran in front of Breeze, where he did not have to fear Strider's nips and Roamer's shoves. The pack was headed for the banks of a frozen river, where they hoped to find moose who had come to graze on willow twigs and branches.

As the wolves ran, streaks appeared overhead. At first, Granite ignored them, then he paused and fell out of line. Planting his feet in the snow, he threw back his head and stared.

The heavens blazed with color. Green streamers spread across the sky, pulled back and spread wide once more. Bands of red, yellow, and green appeared. The banners of light pulsed across the sky like writhing snakes.

Granite was amazed at the display, but the wolves paid little attention. They had seen it many times before. In the strange light, Granite could see the wolves strung out before him, dark against the glistening snow. Breeze had stopped so the dog could enjoy the sight, but soon she urged him on. They hurried to catch up with the running pack.

Long before Granite could make out the clumps of willow, Ebony stopped, turned toward the river, and raised his head. His ears went forward. Sniffing deeply, he stared into the night.

The rest of the pack turned in the same direction. Carried by the wind, the scent of moose filled their heads.

Ebony consulted briefly with the wolves, then advanced toward the source of the smell. They followed, tails wagging. Granite could feel excitement spread along the line of running wolves. His mouth suddenly grew dry. Without breaking stride, he grabbed a mouthful of snow.

As they neared the river, Granite saw the black mass of willow on the far bank. The moose were there. To reach them, the pack would have to cross to the other side.

Now close to the prey, Ebony slowed his pace. Peering intently ahead, he led the wolves onto the ice. At this point, the river was so wide that the whole pack, loping single file, was on the river at one time.

Ebony chose his path with care, traveling where the snow lay thick. He was only a few strides from the far bank when he hit an icy patch, where the wind had blown away the snow cover. He slipped, fell heavily on his shoulder, and slid three wolf-lengths.

Snowdrift, who was behind him, slipped but did not fall. The other wolves, warned by Ebony's tumble, slowed. With toes spread wide, they picked their way across the icy section and up the other side.

Ebony got to his feet, his coat matted with snow. With care, he moved across the ice. As he climbed the bank, he whimpered.

Snowdrift was at his side, whining with concern.

She licked his face, then nosed his body. When she touched his left shoulder, Ebony yelped.

The commotion alerted the moose. They got to their feet but did not flee. Shoulder to shoulder, they stood in the willow grove, dark forms looming above the dark bushes. Motionless, they watched. There were more moose than wolves.

The pack gathered around the big black wolf. He motioned, indicating that they should get on with the hunt.

The wolves started toward the moose. Snowdrift trotted along the river bank, ahead of Roamer and Granite. Strider led Breeze and Climber along the far side of the willow thicket. Unable to keep up, Ebony followed at a distance.

In a few seconds, they reached the moose. Snowdrift and Strider paused, heads down. The moose stared impassively at the wolves. They stared back.

The pack waited. They watched for signs of faltering, hoping to discover a sick or injured animal. If the moose stood their ground, the wolves would look elsewhere for dinner.

At last one of the moose bolted. The snow was so deep that, for the first few steps, the moose struggled on its knees.

The wolves broke into a run. Plunging through

snow that reached their chests, they moved faster than the moose. As the distance narrowed, a feeling of certain victory swept over the excited pack.

The moose burst free of the thicket. In a few steps, it reached a place where the snow was not so deep. With firm footing, the moose's pace quickened.

Suddenly Climber sprinted ahead of Strider. With a great leap, he threw himself at the moose.

His move came as a surprise. Snowdrift and Strider should have attacked first. No one understood why Climber broke ranks. Perhaps he was trying to show his father that he was ready to lead a hunt. Perhaps he thought that, with Ebony disabled, he was needed. Perhaps his reckless nature overcame his allegiance to pack rules.

The attack might have worked. But just as Climber sprang at the moose, it wheeled about and lashed out with its forelegs. The sharp hooves struck Climber in the head. He collapsed in the snow. As Granite watched in disbelief, Climber struggled once to rise, then sank back.

All thoughts of the hunt left the dog's mind. Ignoring the moose, he ran to Climber's still form. Granite licked his face, but the wolf did not respond. There was a deep depression between his eyes, where the deadly hoof had struck.

The moose spread its legs wide, and waited for another attack. None came.

The pack pulled back. Ebony never attacked a fighting moose, and neither Snowdrift nor Strider would do so.

Frightened by Climber's stillness, Granite looked around for Snowdrift. She was already at his side. After sniffing Climber's head, she tried to rouse him with her tongue. He did not move.

Snowdrift threw back her head and howled in despair. Another of her children was gone.

17. Runaway

Each afternoon when Granite awoke, he looked about for Climber. And each afternoon, when Granite remembered that the young wolf was dead, sadness rushed over him. He missed his playmate with the husky face. He missed his only friend among the wolves.

When Granite grew lonely, pictures of his brothers filled his head. He always saw them as small puppies, but they were puppies no more. He wondered if they raced with other dogs. When he thought of Cricket, Granite always saw the bearded stranger and shuddered.

The pictures in Granite's head were fading. Each time he thought about his family, it was harder to see them. Yet his mother's face sometimes was clear. It filled Granite's thoughts when he drank from a still pool and saw a dog in the water. As he stared at the dog's blue eyes, it was like looking into his mother's face. At such times he remembered feeling safe and warm and loved. When Granite wondered if his mother had new babies, he felt cold and lost.

Granite's feelings were all mixed up, because he loved Snowdrift, too. He had been with the wolves for so long that often he forgot that he was a dog. With Climber gone, the wolves would not let him forget.

No matter how hard Granite tried, he could not please Ebony. He was too slow to keep up with the long-legged wolves, and when the pack chased game, he often got in the way. Ebony never bit him, but the big leader often snorted with disgust at the dog's blunders. Breeze ignored him, and Strider and Roamer punished him for every mistake he made — and often for things he did not do. Only Snowdrift was kind.

One day, while the pack slept in the gray dusk of a winter afternoon, Granite ran away. During the night's hunt, he had stumbled in front of Roamer, and the black wolf became angry and nipped Granite's shoulder. The day before Strider had shoved him hard, sending him tumbling down a snowbank. Suddenly it all seemed too much for the dog to bear.

He looked around. Snowdrift was curled beside him with her tail over her nose. Her back was toward him, and she whined in her sleep. Perhaps she was dreaming of her lost pups. It was a mournful sound, and it made Granite feel even sadder.

He got up quietly and crept across the snow-covered rocks and into the trees. As soon as he was out of sight, he began to run. Granite didn't know where he was running. He only knew that he never wanted to see Roamer and Strider again.

Granite could not run as fast as the wolves, but he could run a long time without tiring. He ran and ran. He ran so far that he passed the last of the spots where Ebony or Snowdrift had marked the trail. He ran through the dark until he reached country where the pack had never come.

Still Granite ran on. Above him, the sky was filled with blazing lights. The exploding colors raced across the sky and lifted his spirits. He felt almost happy. His tail rose in the air, and there was no one to nip his neck for the offense.

When Granite grew tired, he found a large, bushy spruce that had fallen across the ground. It was still fresh, and the dense branches formed a safe hiding place. When the dog crawled beneath them, no one could see him.

Making a warm bed, Granite dug into the snow. He had not dug far before he smelled mouse. During the winter, mice stay below the snow and often don't bother to tunnel into the earth. With hopes of food dancing in his head, Granite scratched down to the soil. The mouse was gone. In the place where the mouse had been, Granite found the creature's winter store of fat, white roots. He was so weary that instead of hunting, he ate them.

The dog slept heavily and woke to the dim light of a winter day. The light was so brief that he stayed in his hiding place until dark returned.

It was time to hunt. Granite thought about how he would get his dinner. Without help, there was no way for him to bring down any large game. He trotted with his nose close to the snow, hoping to come across a few mice. Granite was so intent on the search that he almost missed his big chance.

The air was still and no wind passed along the scent. But when Granite raised his head, he saw an enormous flock of ptarmigan feeding in the snow. In their white winter feathers, they looked like snowballs strewn across the clearing.

The dog got down on his stomach and squirmed slowly across the ground, just as he and Climber used to do when scaring ducks. Granite was so careful that it took him an age to move close.

Once he was near the flock, he waited and waited, his muscles tense. Then he sprang. Wings whirred about him, and the birds burst into flight. But one ptarmigan had not been quick enough. Granite's dinner lay trapped beneath his paws, and he was happy to get it.

For a few days, Granite did well on his own. He was no longer the puppy who could not hunt. Besides an occasional ptarmigan or grouse, he ate mice and snowshoe hares and occasionally some dry grass or frozen berries. He was never stuffed, but he had enough to eat.

At first Granite gloried in his freedom. He played in the snow. He scattered sleeping birds. He ran across fields and through forests. He hunted when he was hungry and rested when he was tired. He no longer had to cower before other wolves but walked proudly with his tail held high.

Yet as the days passed, the dog began to yearn for company. He thought about Snowdrift's kindness. He thought of Ebony's wisdom and the stern, but fair way he directed life in the pack. He thought of the excitement of the hunt, when all the wolves worked together like a single animal. A black cloud of loneliness began to grow inside him.

One night Granite came across a caribou haunch buried beneath the snow. The meat was hard and cold, but it filled his stomach. He had been gnawing on it for a long time when a howl rose into the dark sky, held steady for a moment, then wavered and fell.

The fur over Granite's shoulders stood up. Ever since he left Ebony's country, he had been aware that there were wolves somewhere about. The trails he ran across were marked with a scent he did not know. That meant he was in the land of another pack, for each wolf pack has its own territory.

A second howl echoed through the night. Then a third wolf took up the cry. As the wolves drew near, the calls grew louder. Granite knew that he had uncovered a food cache left by the pack of strangers.

As the first wolf came over the crest of the hill, Granite dropped the bone he had been chewing and stood up. A gray wolf with a black face ran down the slope, followed by three others. Two were brown and the third was black. The gray wolf was almost as large as Ebony and his tail waved in the air.

Without a sound, the wolves surrounded Granite. He stood in the center of a circle and waited while they sniffed at him. Granite was careful to keep his tail down.

One of the brown wolves wagged his tail. Granite wagged his tail in return. His hopes rose. Perhaps the wolves would let him join their pack. Then he would no longer be alone.

Suddenly the gray wolf growled, a low, rumbling sound. The hair over his shoulders made a great ruff. The brown wolf stopped wagging his tail and, with ears pointed forward, thrust his head at Granite. The gray wolf's tail, which he carried in a high curve, stiffened and became almost straight.

Granite was in danger. Quickly, he rolled over on his back and threw back his head. He wanted to show the leader that he respected the gray wolf's authority.

The growls did not stop. Then the other wolves joined in. The sound continued for a long time.

The gray wolf straddled Granite, his head down and his lips drawn back to expose his sharp teeth. Granite could see his red gums. Snarling, he snapped at Granite, but his teeth closed on air.

Then the black wolf, a small female who had been watching the gray wolf closely, sprang at the dog. She fastened her teeth onto Granite's front leg, which he had drawn up to protect his throat. When she let go, her fangs were stained with Granite's blood. Excited, the other wolves began to bite at him.

Granite scrambled to his feet. With a sudden burst of strength born of desperation, he pushed his way through the forest of snapping jaws and bolted.

The wolves came after him. Because of their long legs, they had no trouble keeping up. One of the brown wolves knocked him over. Granite fell heavily to the ground, and the breath rushed out of him. He gasped, struggled up and ran again. He had not taken three steps before the gray wolf hit him hard, sending him tumbling.

Again Granite got up, and again he ran. The wolves followed, sinking their sharp teeth into the dog's back at every opportunity.

At last, the pursuing pack let him go. He did not look back. Granite knew that if he stopped, they would kill him. He also knew that he must leave the pack's territory.

Granite ran until he had no more strength. When he could go no farther, he climbed a low rise. Just below the crest, he found a sheltered place among the rocks where he could keep watch for hostile wolves. His back was raw, where they had bitten him repeatedly, and the hair was matted with blood. His leg ached, and he did not know how he had been able to run so far on it. Granite licked his wounds, cleaning them as best he could. Then he made his lonely bed and slept. As his eyes closed, he thought of Snowdrift.

The arrival of gray light woke him briefly, but Granite stayed in the shelter and slept again. He slept for a long time. When at last he stood, every part of his body was stiff.

Slowly, Granite retraced his path to Ebony's country. He had nowhere else to go.

18. The Runaway Returns

Once again the moon was full. It rode low in a clear sky, casting shadows across the snow. With slow steps, Granite traveled back down the trail, putting more distance between him and the angry pack. His heart was heavy and his tail drooped listlessly. He no longer feared being chased, but he had no place to go. His attempt to live on his own had failed.

The land he moved over was the land he had crossed with such joy beneath blazing skies only a few weeks before. His joy had vanished, and he did not know what to do except return to Ebony's country.

The wolves who hunted this land would never let him stay. Their attack had been so vicious that Granite did not even try to cross their territory to places on the other side, where the wolves might be friendly.

It took him a long time to leave this unfriendly land, because he moved only during the light when he knew the hostile pack would be asleep. Granite could not travel fast. His leg was stiff and his back was sore, where a patch of skin was missing at the base of his tail. The moon had crossed the sky three times since he fled, but Granite was still in dangerous territory.

He pushed on. The light was fading when he caught the whisper of a familiar scent. Granite sniffed hard, then ran toward a large rock beside the trail. Eagerly, he drew in great gulps of the smell. It was Ebony's marker.

Granite sighed with relief. His steps quickened. He was surprised that the familiar smell made him feel so good. It brought pictures of Ebony and Snowdrift and the other wolves streaming into his head. He forgot the pain caused by Strider and Roamer. He forgot everything except Snowdrift's kind eyes and caressing tongue.

Granite knew the pack was nowhere near. The scent was old, so old that the moon had grown large and shrunk several times since Ebony had marked the rock.

For the first time since Granite began his flight, he traveled on through the dark. Now that he was back in Ebony's territory, he was safe from the hostile wolves. Each step took him closer to Snowdrift.

Even so, Granite was uneasy. He did not know what Ebony would do at his return. The pack leader had never shown him any affection. Although Ebony might let Granite follow the pack, the black wolf might not be so forgiving. He might attack the dog, as the other wolves had done. Granite was no longer a small puppy, spared to ease Snowdrift's grief.

Despite his fears, Granite kept moving, searching for the pack. Each day the scent markers grew stronger. As he drew close to the pack, Granite began to travel only during the brief periods of light. He was so unsure of his reception that he did not want to meet the pack at a kill.

One gray twilight Granite came across a patch of snow covered with fresh wolf tracks. They crossed and recrossed the prints of a running moose, which kept changing direction. The scents told the dog that the entire pack had chased the moose.

The hunt had not gone well. There was a trampled space where the moose had turned and fought. Then the moose tracks went in one direction and the wolf prints in the other.

Darkness fell and the tracks disappeared, but

Granite followed the trail with his nose. The pack had run through the forest and across a wide, frozen river. As he scrambled up the bank on the far side, he picked up odors from the sleeping wolves.

Yelping softly with excitement, Granite followed the scent, loping at first, then sprinting as the smell grew strong. It was not long before he saw the pack above him, curled up on a rocky promontory that was sheltered by several trees.

Granite did not know what to do. He hesitated. The wind was blowing toward him, carrying his scent away from the pack. It would not do to blunder in among sleeping wolves.

He decided to announce his presence by howling. Before he made a sound, he sniffed deeply. To his surprise, Snowdrift was not with the pack. Without her to protect him, he was in enormous danger. Granite turned and trotted back along the trail.

He had gone only a few feet before he was stopped by a howl. Someone had spotted him. He looked over his shoulder and saw Strider, standing on the highest rock. The gray wolf stared at Granite, then opened his mouth wide and howled again.

All the wolves were on their feet now, dark shapes against the sky. It was like that spring night so long ago when Granite first encountered the pack. But this time there was no Snowdrift to speak for him.

It would do no good to run. Granite threw back his head and sent his friendliest greeting into the sky.

First one, then another of the wolves answered him. They began to pace restlessly back and forth. Roamer, Strider, and Breeze gathered around Ebony, yelping with excitement and nuzzling the big black wolf.

Granite waited in mounting fear.

Ebony stepped out of the circle and spoke. It was a deep, throaty howl that grew louder, turned into a bark that was almost a growl, then became a howl again. He bounded down from the promontory, leaping from rock to rock. When he reached level ground, he stood waiting for Granite. The wolf's legs were stiff and his tail arched over his back.

Granite dropped his tail and pulled back his ears. As the dog moved toward the pack leader, he bobbed his head, first moving it up and down, then from side to side. He tried desperately to show how sorry he was that he had run away from the pack. Still a wolf's length from the leader, Granite stopped.

Ebony walked to where Granite stood cringing. The long-legged wolf loomed over the smaller dog, who was careful not to make a sound. Ebony stared at Granite for a long time. He seemed to be deciding what to do with the runaway.

Granite turned his head and looked up at Ebony. An angry fire burned in the wolf's brown eyes. In the moment before Granite dropped his gaze, he felt that he was looking into a blazing sun.

Granite's heart beat against his side like a trapped bird. He rolled onto his back and lifted his leg.

Ebony growled.

Granite's fear was so great that he could not move. He waited.

The other wolves fell silent. They were waiting, too.

Ebony lowered his great head until it was beside Granite's face. Then he opened his jaws. His long white teeth glistened in the moonlight. They closed on Granite's muzzle. It was not a hard bite. Ebony had decided to let the dog live.

Until the air rushed out of Granite's chest, he did not know that he had been holding his breath. He licked Ebony's mouth and whined his thanks. Then he got to his feet, making certain that his tail stayed down.

The pack was bound by Ebony's judgment. Whether they agreed with their leader made no difference. Forced to let Granite return to the pack, the wolves ran down to greet the dog. Growling and yapping, they shoved him around and nipped his nose, his shoulders, and his legs.

Keeping his ears back and his tail low, Granite accepted the bites. None of them drew blood. They were the wolves' way of reminding Granite that he was still the lowest of the low.

There was a sudden commotion, and a white body burst through the wolves clustered around Granite. It was Snowdrift. As if he were still a small puppy, she cracked him with the side of her head.

Granite's head rang with the force of the blow. He raised his front paw and licked at Snowdrift's muzzle.

Her anger was gone. She had punished Granite for leaving and was ready to go on with their lives.

19. *Searching for Snowdrift*

Life in the pack went on as it had before Granite left. Now that the dog knew the loneliness and danger of a solitary life, he accepted the blows and nips of Roamer and Strider. He still hoped to please Ebony, but he wondered if that day would ever come.

The weather grew mild. During the day, the snow was soft, but at night the top froze into a hard crust that made traveling easy. The lakes and rivers were still thick with ice, but on the small creeks, water had begun to flow.

It would soon be spring. Granite climbed a rise and saw a bear digging for roots on the mountain slope, her club playing beside her. Then he saw a flight of swans, as white as new-fallen snow, spread across the cloudless, blue sky. Everywhere there were birds — black-headed chickadees, red-headed finches, noisy jays, and big, red-breasted robins.

Ever since the first robin appeared, Snowdrift had been restless. She knew that it was time for the birth of pups, but there were none in the pack this year.

Late in the morning she often disappeared and was gone for hours. Ebony behaved as if nothing were wrong, as if she had gone looking for small game. That was something any member of the pack might do. Yet all the wolves and even Granite knew the hunt was not for hare or squirrels, but for her lost pups.

Although Snowdrift knew the pups were gone forever, she still spent her days searching for them. Each day she hoped to find her babies and each time she failed, she grieved anew.

One evening Snowdrift did not come back. She had never stayed away so long before. As the sun sank low in the sky, Ebony paced restlessly on the ledge that overlooked the pack's resting place. He walked back and forth, back and forth.

Tired of play, the wolves settled silently on their haunches. Their eyes followed Ebony's movements.

Darkness fell. Black clouds covered the moon and a cold wind blew across the snowy fields.

Ebony peered into the night. There was nothing to see but branches bending in the wind. His ears stood erect and he tilted his head, straining for sounds of Snowdrift's return.

There was nothing to hear but the soft hoot of an owl, getting ready to make its nightly search for food. Ebony stretched his neck and sniffed deeply. There was nothing to smell but the familiar scents of the resting place.

Granite lay still, his nose on his paws, watching Ebony. The leader tried to hide his fears, but the pack could smell them. They were sharper than the scent of mouse, stronger than the odor of squirrel. The smell made the hair on Granite's back stand up and sent uneasy prickles down his spine.

At last Ebony howled for the hunt to begin. The song that floated across the clearing was full of uneasy notes. When the last howls died away, the wolves started down the trail.

The hunt went poorly. Five times they stalked a caribou and five times they failed to bring it down. Though they covered many miles, they had only two squirrels and an Arctic hare to show for their labor.

Hoping to find Snowdrift, Ebony led the pack

back to the place where they had slept the day before. The resting place was empty.

Everyone was in a bad humor. It was time for the pack to sleep in the shade, but no one felt like sleeping. No one felt like playing, either. The wolves walked restlessly, back and forth, but no one walked near Ebony.

Strider went out of his way to cross Granite's path. As he passed, he snapped and knocked the dog sprawling with a heavy paw. Granite hid behind Breeze and peered cautiously around her legs. She stepped away as if the dog were not there.

Ebony was back on the ridge. He stood, staring into the distance, as if he expected to see Snowdrift appear at any moment.

At last he jumped down and howled for the pack. They stood nose to nose, waiting for Ebony's signal.

He howled again, then loped down the trail. The pack fell in line behind him, but no tails wagged. The wolves knew they were not hunting. They were on their way to the old meadow, where Snowdrift had last seen her pups.

All day they traveled, trotting in the spring sun. Despite the snow on the ground, they panted in the heat, their mouths open and their tongues hanging out. Ebony set such a fast pace that Granite's legs grew tired.

At last the pack reached the stream that flowed past a broad meadow. By now dusk was gathering.

The wolves followed Ebony along the stream bank until he signaled that it was time to rest. He lay down beneath a clump of willows. Granite and the wolves found comfortable spots and curled up to sleep.

Ebony did not rest long. He jumped up and began to pace, just as he had the day before when Snowdrift did not return. He came over to where Breeze and Granite were dozing.

He looked down at them. He nudged Breeze's paws and saw that they were sore. He sniffed Granite's mouth. He knew that the pack could go no farther.

Ebony found another spot and lay down, but he did not close his eyes. The last thing Granite saw before he fell asleep was Ebony on his feet again, staring down the trail.

20. The Hunt

The drone of a plane's engine filled the air above the winding river. The river and the twin lakes to its east were solid and silent with ice.

The plane was on a day trip out of Fairbanks, carrying two vacationing hunters from the lower forty-eight. They were searching for wolves. The pilot, who was also the guide, had chosen this valley because it was a place where caribou came to calve. The calving would not begin for a few weeks, but the cows had begun to congregate. Their presence was sure to attract wolf packs.

This trip was the last hunt of the season over snow. Within days, the white covering would vanish and spotting wolves from the air would be difficult.

As the plane moved through the morning sky, the hunters swapped stories about the vicious ways of wolves. The hunter in the green anorak described a dog's death the previous year.

"Old Butch was sleeping on the back porch," said the big man, brushing back the soft wolverine fur around his face. "He was a tough old dog but never had a chance. Those wolves just chewed him up and swallowed him down." His blue eyes shone with excitement. "All they ever found of him was a few scraps of hide."

The other hunter nodded. "Wolves are mean critters," he said. "Best thing we can do is get rid of them. If we could wipe out the wolves, the country would be teeming with moose and caribou."

The pilot said nothing. He knew the story of Old Butch. The wolves had killed him all right, but only after his owner chained him up outside for the night. Poor dog had no way to run and couldn't defend himself. Hunters from the lower forty-eight were full of stories that were half-true or never happened.

The second hunter, a small man with brown eyes and the beginnings of a beard, tapped the pilot on the shoulder. "Ever hear about the wolf that attacked the little girl over by Takotna?" he asked.

"No," said the pilot. "Matter of fact, there's never been a case of wolves attacking humans in Alaska.

They see people, they go the other way. They're smart animals."

The bearded hunter frowned and braced himself as a swirling eddy of air jolted the plane. "That's not the way I heard it," he said.

The pilot bit off each word. "That's the way it is."

The hunter fell silent. He rubbed his chin, satisfied at the rasping sound of whiskers under his thumb.

Suddenly, the hunter in the green anorak leaned forward. "There!" he said. "Just ahead of us. Look!"

Below them, a white form was climbing a gray rock that jutted out of the snow.

"What is it?" asked the bearded hunter. "A polar bear?"

The pilot laughed. "No polar bears this far south. It's a wolf — a white one."

"I thought wolves were gray," said the hunter.

"Most of them are gray or black," said the pilot, "but sometimes we see a white one."

He pushed the controls forward and the nose of the plane dipped. The ground rushed up toward them.

"We can land on that meadow ahead," he said, "and you can start your hunt."

"Land first? And let that critter get away? No,

sir!" The hunter in the green anorak picked up his loaded shotgun and threw off the safety. He turned the window latch and pushed open the glass.

"Don't!" said the pilot. "It's against the law to shoot wolves from a plane."

"Forget the law," said the hunter.

The white wolf was directly ahead of them. It raised its head and they could see its yellow eyes.

The hunter took careful aim. Just as he pulled the trigger, the pilot swerved the plane sharply.

As his shots went wide, the hunter cursed.

Below him the wolf bounded off the rock and ran across the meadow, making for a clump of trees. Against the white snow, its coat looked yellow.

Before the wolf reached the trees, the gun spoke again. Twice. The wolf leaped into the air and fell heavily into the snow.

"Let's go down and get him," said the bearded hunter.

"No way," said the pilot. He was furious. "There's probably a ranger over the next rise. Want me to lose my license?"

There was no ranger within fifty miles, but the pilot was determined not to let the hunters profit from their illegal shots. The wolf was probably a goner, but maybe not. At least he'd give it a chance.

Something about wolf hunters bothered the pilot. They were different from the men who went after moose or caribou or salmon. And when they broke the law, they put him squarely on the side of the hunted. That wasn't hard to do. He always hated to see a prime animal brought down or a record fish reeled in. He recalled the times he'd taken fishermen after salmon and deliberately tied their leaders with slip knots. When a big salmon leaped, the knot unraveled and the fish swam free.

The plane roared up and away. The sound of its engine faded. On the snowy field below, the white wolf lay in the place where it fell. It did not move.

21. A Sad Discovery

It was still dark when Breeze nudged Granite awake. The rest of the pack were on their feet, roused by Ebony's howl. Granite was so tired that he had slept through the commotion.

Slowly, the dog got up and stretched. His pads were still tender, but the stiffness had left his legs. He scampered over to the spring and lapped up the water that flowed above the ice.

It was the time when the pack usually was deep into the hunt, but Ebony did not start a hunting song. Instead, he turned on his heel and trotted away without a sound. The wolves followed, as they always did.

As Breeze and Granite swung into line, Strider warned the dog not to lag behind. Ebony would not rest again until he had reached the old meadow.

Granite made a game of the trip, pretending that

when he reached the second blueberry bush along the trail he would get a fat snowshoe hare for his dinner. That made him run fast.

Granite counted blueberry bushes until he grew tired, but there was no hare that night. Not even a single mouse. No one took the time to search for food. The wolves trotted silently, heads down, on their worrisome journey.

The pack moved quickly, through trees, up rises, and down hillsides, following the stream. Now and again an owl hooted or a bush crackled as some animal got out of their way.

The hours wore on. The darkness of night became gray, then pink. As the sun rose behind them, the line of wolves neared the old meadow. It lay on the other side of the next rise.

Ebony broke into a run. His powerful legs carried him over the crest of the hill and out of sight.

The rest of the pack kept at their steady pace, but before they reached the hilltop, a sorrowful howl cut through the morning air. It rose higher and higher, trembled, and died away. Something was wrong.

Strider and Roamer sprinted up the hill and were gone. Breeze ran part way, then darted back to Granite. She urged him to hurry.

The dog did his best, but his legs were so tired that they could hardly move.

At last Breeze and Granite reached the top and began the journey down the other side. They moved a little faster now. They threaded their way among the rocks and around the bushes. The meadow lay before them, in the cup at the base of the hill.

Suddenly Breeze was gone. Granite raised his head. Below him the wolves were clustered together, looking at something. Breeze joined them.

The wind blowing up the hill brought strong smells of fear and blood. Granite's fur stood up, making a ruff down his back. His stomach twisted. He was frightened, but he didn't know why. He forgot his weariness and ran down the slope at full speed, seeking the safety of the pack.

Granite reached the bottom of the hill, but no one noticed him. They were intent on something.

He slipped through the legs of the big wolves, but no one snapped or snarled. Even Strider paid no attention to the dog. His eyes did not waver from whatever was before him in the snow.

There, in a heap, lay a bundle of white fur. It was Snowdrift. Her eyes were closed and her breath came in great, shuddering sighs. On her side, the fur was stiff with dried blood and there were heavy clots at the base of her skull. Around her, patches of blood stained the snow.

Granite whimpered with fear.

Ebony howled again, and the other wolves joined in. In the silence that followed his cry, he licked Snowdrift's wounds. When he had cleaned the blood away, he motioned for help.

Together, the wolves moved Snowdrift toward the shade of some willow bushes. Strider and Ebony gripped her hind legs delicately in their mouths and gently tugged at her. Breeze and Roamer and Granite nudged her with their noses. Slowly, they dragged her across the snow.

Snowdrift whined with pain. Her eyes opened but they were blank. She struggled wildly to get up. As she picked up the scent of the pack, she relaxed and sank back to the ground.

The wolves shoved her under the willows, where she lay, panting heavily.

Snowdrift needed water. The wolves scooped snow and carried it in their mouths to where Snowdrift lay. Standing over her, each wolf and Granite released melting snow on her muzzle.

Weakly, Snowdrift's tongue licked up a few drops. Again and again, the pack brought mouthfuls of melting snow. Again and again, Snowdrift lapped it up. Then she slept.

Ebony sniffed her neck, her ears, and her muzzle. Then he lay down beside her. The rest of the pack lay down, too. The wolves slept fitfully until the world grew dark and a small, silver moon climbed the sky — all except Ebony, who watched over his mate with worried eyes.

22. *The Ice Pack*

For many days, Snowdrift lay helpless, blind and unable to walk. One bullet had creased her skull and another had struck her in the side and passed through, leaving a deep wound on both sides of her body.

Except when he was leading the hunt, Ebony stayed close by. He treated Snowdrift as if she were a puppy, cleansing her wound and bringing her morsels of meat. Her bed was close to the stream, and the wolves took turns carrying water.

While Snowdrift was helpless, the pack hunted less often. The melting snow uncovered the frozen bodies of animals that had failed to survive the winter, and the hillsides teemed with young lambs and caribou calves. The wolves kept plenty of meat around their resting place so that Snowdrift would never be hungry. Ever since they had settled in the old meadow, their stomachs had been pleasantly full.

The days grew long and new grass covered the meadow. The mountain slopes turned green. Willow leaves unfurled and buds opened on the cottonwoods. Blueberries bloomed nearby, and violets grew along the stream. Pink wallflowers and roses surrounded Snowdrift's bed. Even though she couldn't see the flowers, she could smell them.

Swollen with melted snow, the creeks threatened to spill over their banks. Water poured into the river, where streams ran between a fringe of ice along the shore and the solid ice in the center.

One day, while the pack was resting, Granite trotted along the stream and down the river. Big trees grew along the narrow, twisting course. Here the river had undercut the bank until the tree trunks tilted and their branches swept far over the water.

Granite ran along the bank until he came to a place where a rushing stream entered the river. Below the stream, the solid sheet of ice had broken into large pieces separated by narrow water passages. As he trotted downstream, the breeze brought the scent of snowshoe hare. It came from across the water.

Granite wasn't hungry, but he never missed a

chance to practice his hunting skills. All winter the pack had crossed and recrossed frozen rivers and creeks. Without a second thought, Granite jumped onto a large slab of ice and began to leap from floe to floe.

The ice was moving downstream, but so slowly that even a short-legged dog could make the jumps. As Granite worked his way across, the channels between the ice shrank.

He had reached the other bank when a noise like thunder rang through the valley. He looked upstream and saw a pile of ice. It was as big as a small hill.

Sitting back on his haunches, Granite watched as the hill became a mountain of ice and moved slowly downstream. Great pieces rolled and heaved, pushing other pieces before them. With sounds like distant thunder, the ice pack piled up.

Never before had the dog seen such a sight, but the enticing smell of hare pulled him away. He forgot the strange stacks of ice and trotted off after the hare. He followed the hare for a long time. Then the wind shifted and he lost the scent.

With the fading of the scent, Granite's prospects for dinner vanished. By now he knew enough about hunting to realize that without the smell to guide him, he would never spot his prey. A snowshoe hare can sit all day without moving, and its coat blends into the landscape. Upwind of a hare, a dog or a wolf could pass within a few inches and never see it. Sadly, Granite turned back to the river.

The ice now filled the river from bank to bank and had come to a halt. It had become a groaning, cracking mountain of ice.

As Granite picked his way across the ice, there was a mighty explosion, louder than he had ever heard before. The river roared to life, breaking the jam. Ice surged over the banks, flattening brush and uprooting trees. The ice moved faster than a wolf walks.

It took Granite a moment to realize that he was in danger. When he did, all thoughts of fat hares fled. He ran toward shore, jumping from one slab of ice to the next.

The ice was carrying him downstream, but Granite no longer cared where he reached land. As his feet came down on one great chunk of ice, it began to turn beneath him. The dog scrambled for a foothold, but his paws slipped. Cold water flowed over his hind feet.

He struggled to get back onto the ice, but he could feel water rushing over his legs and tail. In another moment he would be crushed between grinding chunks of ice.

Granite was ready to give up when he looked toward shore. There, watching silently from a flat rock above the river, was Strider. The gray wolf did not move.

Granite remembered the porcupine hunt. Anger surged through him. With a final desperate heave, he pulled himself out of the water and onto the slab of ice. As he struggled to his feet, the ice beneath him tilted. He began sliding toward the water. Before the slab could roll again, he jumped to the next chunk.

Two more leaps and there was earth beneath Granite's feet. He sprawled on the grass, unable to take another step. He gasped for air. The beating of his heart seemed louder than thunder.

When his heart slowed, Granite looked upstream toward the flat rock. It was empty.

By the time Granite returned to the resting place, the pack was playing in the twilight. Breeze and Roamer were chasing Strider. As he ran by, he turned his head. His brown eyes stared into Granite's. His gaze oozed contempt.

That gaze chilled Granite to the heart. It told him that Strider had expected him to drown. The gray wolf was no stranger to ice jams. He knew their power. Yet he watched the dog start across the river without a warning bark. He simply watched, waiting for Granite to be swept to his death.

In silence, Granite regarded the playing wolves. Since he had come to live with the pack, the seasons had passed and it was spring once more. He had been with the wolves for nearly a year, and he was no longer a helpless pup. Yet Strider hated him as much as he did the first night when Snowdrift presented the pack with a frightened, injured puppy. That evening Granite hunted with a heavy heart.

23. Breeze Battles a Salmon

The days grew long and hot. Patches of color covered the green mountain slopes. When the wolves traveled up toward the ridges where sheep grazed, they ran through clumps of yellow, pink, orange, blue, and white flowers. Here they could always find cool breezes, coming from mountain peaks that never lost their snowy cover.

All that summer, the pack stayed in the meadow. Snowdrift was too weak to hunt, but she no longer needed constant care. She made her way alone, walking slowly to the stream to drink and eating at the pack's caches near the meadow.

So much small game roamed the fields and forest that summer that the wolves rarely hunted as a pack. Instead, two or three would go off together, looking for ground squirrel, marmot, or hare. And there was always a mouse or vole to be snatched from the grassy meadow.

Every day Granite hoped that Ebony would take him along, but the big wolf never did. Usually, he took Roamer or Strider, but sometimes Breeze was at his side. Granite wanted to show the leader that he could be a good hunter, but he never got the chance.

Only Breeze ever let Granite accompany her. Since Snowdrift's injury, Breeze had been almost kind to the dog. She was never affectionate, but she had become tolerant and sometimes helped him with his tracking skills.

One hot afternoon she took Granite along when she went in search of food. As the pair trotted along the trail, looking for a careless squirrel, Breeze froze. The air was still. Not a bird sang.

Breeze sniffed hard, and so Granite sniffed, too. A strong, musky odor filled his nose. He had smelled it before, and the scent made him tremble.

At the sound of breaking branches, Granite looked to the right. A big brown bear sat in a clump of blueberry bushes. She was as big as a whole pack of wolves. Granite caught his breath.

The bear's head swung slowly back and forth, up and down. She ate the plump berries as fast as she could. Her long tongue slid over the branches, stripping off leaves as well as berries.

She feasted in silence, her mouth stained with berry juice. The sounds Granite heard were not hers. They were made by her young cub, who clumsily imitated his mother. He broke off branches, and as many twigs as berries went into his mouth.

The bears paid no attention to the wolf. Breeze settled back on her haunches and watched them eat. Granite imitated Breeze, sitting just as straight and as still as she did. The memory of the charging bear made his fur stand on end, but he pretended he was used to seeing enormous grizzlies.

Moving from one bush to another, the bear worked her way through the clump of blueberries and disappeared among the trees, followed by her cub.

Breeze got up, stretched, and started off in the opposite direction. She had given Granite a lesson in the rules of the pack: Don't bother bears and they won't bother you.

The young dog was almost full-grown, but he found it hard to keep his mind on his lessons while over among the willows, a ptarmigan clucked softly to her brood. Granite started to follow Breeze, but he could resist no longer. Away he dashed, with thoughts of tender bird making his mouth water. Before he reached the ptarmigan, they fluttered out of reach.

Breeze shook her head. She let Granite know that he was not much of a hunter. Wolves did not tell the whole world that they were on the way.

Granite's head drooped. He was good at catching mice and sometimes caught a squirrel or a startled ptarmigan that froze instead of flying. But no large animal of any kind had reason to fear him. His nose still smarted when he thought of the porcupine hunt with Strider.

Breeze was intent on giving Granite another lesson. She loped over to the stream.

Granite ran hard to keep up.

Breeze trotted along the bank, then stopped. In the middle of the stream, a broad, flat rock rose out of the water. It was shallow here, but just above the rock was a deep pocket.

The wolf stepped into the water and walked delicately to the rock. She climbed out and stood over the rushing water, her head down and her eyes fixed on the edge of the hole, where the water level dropped and she could see small stones on the bottom. Insects hovered on the surface of the stream.

Granite watched from the bank. He had no idea

what she was doing. The wait seemed an eternity. To one side, he heard the rustle of a squirrel as it ran through the brush toward a nearby tree. He ached to run after it, but he forced himself to remain as still and silent as Breeze.

The sun moved across the cloudless sky, but Breeze waited. Then, when it seemed to Granite that he could stay still no longer, Breeze lunged. Water sprayed high in the air.

The big wolf turned to face Granite. Between her dripping jaws wriggled a fat fish, its sides shining in the sun.

Breeze splashed through the stream and dropped the fish on the bank. It flopped in the grass, its colors fading.

Granite was astonished. He had never before seen a wolf catch a fish. He wondered if he would ever be patient enough to capture such a creature.

24. *Granite Moves Up*

As the weeks passed, Snowdrift's strength returned. She moved freely, without pain. Her eyes were still blank, but her ears and her nose told her all she needed to know. She could hear a mouse rustle in the grass or a hare hopping on spruce needles. When she joined the evening games of tag and chase, she never bumped another wolf or stumbled on rocks in her path. Sometimes it was hard for Granite to believe that she was blind.

The wolves moved and hunted, hunted and moved, just as they had when Snowdrift could see. Had it not been for Roamer and Strider, life in the pack would have been good for Granite that autumn.

The dog had stopped growing, but he was still the smallest member of the pack. His chest was broad and his legs were short and stocky. His neck was short and thick. With their long, slender necks and willowy legs, the wolves towered over him.

Despite Granite's short legs, he was almost as good a hunter as Roamer. He could catch fish from the stream and trap a porcupine without getting a face full of quills. Once he even caught a beaver, who was so absorbed in gnawing at a sapling that he took it by surprise. When he hunted on his own, he had learned to travel in a straight line as wolves do instead of wandering back and forth across the trail dog-fashion, sniffing at every stray scent. He knew how to join in driving prey toward a waiting hunter. He could tell when a moose or caribou was tiring and open to attack. He had learned to search the sky for ravens, who often hovered above distant herds of game, and to listen for their cries.

Although Ebony paid no attention to Granite, he watched the leader carefully and learned some of his hunting tricks. While the pack rested, Granite often went into the woods and practiced the way Ebony turned swiftly, reversing direction and surprising his prey. He also practiced Ebony's special style of stalking animals, moving stealthily through the grass or over the rocks.

Granite learned to stalk so quietly and slowly that he could creep within a wolf's leap of a creature before it knew he was there. He did this even when he was not hungry, making a game of slipping next to an unsuspecting squirrel or fox, then leaping out of the grass with a loud bark. As Granite watched the frightened creature flee, he often thought of Climber and how the young wolf would have enjoyed this game.

On a crisp fall afternoon, Granite started up the slope above the resting place, moving carefully among the orange and scarlet bushes. Pretending that he was Ebony stalking a porcupine, he crouched close to the ground.

Halfway up the slope, he saw a marmot waddling across an open space. Granite caught his breath. In autumn, a marmot was a delicious treat, full of fat stored for the winter. Before the moon grew large again, the creature would be slumbering in its rocky burrow, safe until spring.

Marmots are furry creatures with small ears and short, bushy tails. Their short legs make them so slow that they give wolves a wide berth. This one must have seen the pack below and decided that their slumber made it safe to venture out.

Keeping his eyes on the marmot, Granite crept even more slowly than before. Between each step, he froze and waited until the marmot looked the other way before moving.

The marmot never knew Granite was there. The dog moved so close he feared the marmot could hear him breathe. Then he pounced, grabbed the animal in his jaws, and gave it a mighty shake. Filled with pride, Granite carried the marmot back down the hill. He planned to share the meal with Snowdrift.

Just before Granite reached the pack, Roamer awoke and looked about. He saw Granite, and he smelled the meat the dog carried.

Roamer jumped up and ran toward Granite, his tail held high. With three leaps, he was at Granite's side. The hair on his shoulders bristled and his tail trembled. His brown eyes stared into the blue eyes of the dog. Roamer raised his ears, stretched his legs, and bared his teeth. He growled without stopping for breath.

As the lowest ranking pack member, Granite was supposed to drop his prey at Roamer's feet. Then he was supposed to crouch and back away, with his ears flat and his tail between his legs.

He didn't. Granite's tail and ears rose, and his hair stood high. He stared back at Roamer, trying to look confident. Holding the marmot tightly in his teeth, Granite growled.

Roamer's eyes widened. He looked bewildered. A lowly dog had dared to challenge him. There was a moment of silence, then he snapped at Granite.

Granite dropped his prey. The pair circled about, snarling at each other.

For a moment, they were side by side, and before Granite could move, Roamer lunged at his flank. The dog sidestepped. As he whirled back, he felt the wolf's hot breath and heard the click of his teeth.

Again they circled. Granite watched Roamer closely. He seemed nervous.

The dog rushed at the wolf. Using his heavy chest, Granite shoved hard. Roamer tumbled off his feet.

Opening his jaws wide, Granite leaped for Roamer's neck and fastened his teeth in the wolf's shoulder.

Roamer turned his head to the side and closed his teeth on Granite's ear. The dog felt a stab of pain but did not let go.

The commotion wakened the other wolves. They

gathered around the fighting pair. The wolves made no sound. No one interfered.

Roamer and Granite rolled over and over. Granite wondered how long he could hold on.

Then Roamer's mouth opened. Releasing Granite's ear, he whined.

Granite straddled the wolf and lowered his head. Blood ran down the dog's face and into his eye, but he kept snarling.

Roamer, his ears flat against his head, lay half on his side and half on his back. His paw was drawn up and his belly was exposed. His tail was tucked between his legs.

Holding his tail proudly above his back, Granite stared fiercely at the black wolf who had harassed him for so long.

Roamer whimpered. It was a puppy's whimper, helpless and imploring.

After a few seconds, Granite stopped snarling and licked Roamer's face, letting the wolf know that Granite accepted his submission. Then Granite stepped back.

Roamer got to his feet, keeping his tail between his legs. He licked the side of Granite's face, just as he did with Strider.

With the fight over, the other wolves trotted back down the hill. It made little difference to them who had won, but it made a great difference to Granite.

The dog picked up his marmot and walked away, his head high. Never again would Roamer torment him. Granite had moved up in the pack.

25. Avalanche

It had been three days since the pack had eaten. They were traveling a mountain trail, searching for sheep. While they ran, the sun rose but it soon set again, for the season of snow and darkness had returned. The silent, sparse flakes of the pre-dawn gloom became a raging storm.

Filled with snow swept from the peaks above, the fierce wind formed a whirlpool around the wolves that sucked away the air and left them breathless. Snow blotted out their surroundings, enveloping them in a swirl of white. Stinging snow blew into their eyes and clotted their fur so that all were as pale as Snowdrift.

Everyone was tired. Their paws were sore from the snow and ice collected between their toes. Ice needles formed around their eyes, and if they blinked, their eyelashes froze their eyes shut. Rest seemed more important than food.

At last Ebony found shelter beneath a rocky ledge. The wolves curled up together, their tails over their noses, waiting for the wind to slacken. They waited for a long time.

When Granite finally awoke, the skies were clear and filled with stars. Ebony and Strider had broken through the new snowfall that shut the pack off from the trail and were urging the wolves to their feet. One by one, the wolves rose, stretched their stiff legs, and moved to Ebony's side.

The wind had died and the landscape above the treeline was an unbroken mass of snow. The trail, the rocks, and the bushes had become a smooth silver meadow that stretched down to the valley below.

After touching noses, Ebony took the pack back on the hunt. Each step plunged them into soft snow over their bellies. If their legs had been longer, they would have sunk deeper.

For a long time the wolves struggled through the snow without scenting game. Strider wanted to rest until a crust formed on the snow, but Ebony kept going. Granite was so weary that his legs ached, but he kept silent.

At a signal from Snowdrift, they stopped. No one made a sound. As the wolves watched, Snowdrift raised her head high and sniffed deeply. Then she wheeled and charged into the snow on the left side of the trail. Led by the white wolf, the pack lunged over a rise and along a sheltered slope.

Soon the rest of the pack caught the oily scent of sheep rising from the snow. Digging together, they uncovered the body of an old ram that had died during the great storm. After Ebony and Snowdrift ate, the rest of the pack fell hungrily on what was left. Strider was so famished that, after a single snarl, he let Granite eat in peace. Roamer no longer dared to challenge the dog.

A few days later, as the pack traveled in half-light, they came to a place where a high cliff of glittering snow and ice rose steeply above the trail. The wolves were strung out along the grade, and that day Snowdrift and Granite ran at the end of the line.

All at once, a crack and a rumble shattered the still air. Granite looked up and saw the side of the mountain collapse. What seemed to the dog like all the snow in the world broke loose and came booming down the slope. It was headed straight for them.

Trying to escape the tumbling snow, the pack scattered. Wolves ran in all directions. Snowdrift and Granite plunged down the slope in the hope of outrunning the hurtling chunks.

When they were only a few leaps from the bottom and it looked as if they had beaten the avalanche, Granite began to relax. Then there was another rumble and more snow tore loose from the towering heights.

With an extra burst of speed, Granite reached the foot of the hill and bounded across a gully and up the opposite slope. His heart beat louder than a woodpecker pounding on a spruce trunk, but he ran until the rumbling stopped and the world grew silent.

Panting, Granite looked down the hillside. The wolves were gone. There was nothing but snow before him. He was alone. Granite whimpered like a puppy.

There was no one to help him. He slid down the slope and began to search. Sniffing sharply, Granite ran back and forth across the snow, making wider and wider circles. He was desperate to detect the scent of wolf.

At last he caught a faint odor. He recognized it as Snowdrift's. Furiously, Granite dug toward the smell, sending showers of snow into the air. He dug a hole as deep as he was high. The smell grew stronger. Then Granite heard Snowdrift grunt.

In a few minutes he had reached the white wolf. She was shuddering with fear. She struggled to her feet. Heaving herself slowly out of the snow, she shook the snow from her coat. She was not hurt.

Granite started to search for the scent of other wolves. When Snowdrift stopped trembling, she joined him. They searched for a long time but found nothing. A new mountain of snow covered the trail and separated them from the pack.

Snowdrift gave up the search and turned back. She had remembered the existence of an old cross-trail that ran through the mountains. It would eventually bring them to the trail that was now buried. If the other wolves had escaped, they would find them, probably at one of the resting places.

The pair started off, Snowdrift in the lead. She didn't need her eyes to find the way. Once they were beyond the great snowfall, she put her nose to the ground and followed the familiar scents. Granite stayed close at her heels.

They came to the cross-trail, and without hesitating, Snowdrift swung onto it. They traveled for a long time, winding between hills and down into gullies. The pack had not gone this way for many moons. The scent markers had faded, and Granite could smell only lynx and wolverine. But Snowdrift did not pause. Her sharp nose picked up the old markers.

Before long, the trail wound upward, along the side of a mountain. It took them higher and higher, far above the valley floor. Granite looked around but saw nothing he recognized. He had never been on this trail before.

Then a howl drifted through the air. Snowdrift stopped to listen. Another howl. It was Ebony.

Snowdrift yipped with excitement, then answered his cry. She left the trail, sprinting in the direction of the sound. Granite followed. From time to time, Ebony and Snowdrift exchanged howls.

Snowdrift scrambled up a rise, with Granite close behind. As they started to descend, Granite caught a familiar scent and looked up. He squeaked with joy. There, across a deep gorge, stood the pack. When they saw Snowdrift, they yipped a welcome.

Turning in the direction of their cries, Snowdrift left Granite's side. She bolted through the snow, guided only by the familiar smells and voices.

Before she had gone far, the pack's happy calls changed to cries of warning. Snowdrift neither changed course nor slowed. Suddenly Granite realized that she could not see her danger. Her path had taken her onto a ledge that jutted over the gorge. She was running straight toward the drop.

Barking as loudly as he could, Granite raced to catch her.

Snowdrift paid no attention. Confidently, she approached the edge. Another step would take her into space.

With a flying leap, Granite smashed into her side. As they tumbled over and over, Granite expected at any moment to find himself plunging through the air. At last they stopped.

Granite opened his eyes. He and Snowdrift were lying against a small boulder. On the other side of the rock was emptiness. Far below them, at the bottom of the gorge, wound a silent river of ice.

Snowdrift started to get up.

Granite barked a warning.

She lay back and did not move.

The slightest mistake would tumble them both over the cliff. Moving carefully, Granite got up and edged back from the drop. He braced his feet, then carefully grasped Snowdrift's fur in his teeth. As if he had been moving a puppy, Granite tugged the white wolf away from the gorge.

At first Snowdrift was limp, and it took all Granite's strength to move her the space of a puppy's paw. Then she understood what Granite was doing and pushed against the rock with her feet. They scooted back until they were on safe ground.

Granite whimpered with relief.

While the pair struggled back from the drop, the wolves across the gorge watched them intently. No one made a sound. As soon as both were safe, the pack began barking and howling with joy.

After they caught their breath, Snowdrift followed Granite back over the rise to an old trail that wound down the slope and across the ridge where Granite had seen the pack.

Snowdrift picked up the trail markers and swung into the lead. By the time they reached the waiting wolves, the twilight had faded, and it was night again.

Ebony ran to meet them, his tail wagging. He licked Snowdrift's face. When the pair had finished their greetings, Ebony turned to Granite.

Obeying the rules of the pack, the dog tucked his tail between his legs and lowered his head. To Granite's surprise, Ebony licked his face, too.

The rest of the wolves gathered about, as happy to see them as Ebony had been. Never had their greetings been so enthusiastic. They had watched Granite save Snowdrift's life. Even Strider was friendly and paid no attention to Granite's tail, which had crept high above his back.

It was not long before the pack came upon a ewe that had been separated from the herd. She was downhill from the wolves and could not escape.

They spread out, making ready to charge. For the first time, Ebony did not send Granite to the rear with Snowdrift. Instead, he placed the dog next to him, where Strider usually hunted. Side by side, the pair ran down the slope, leading the attack.

Working together, the pack soon brought down the sheep. They ate well that night.

Later when the pack was resting, Granite looked up to see Strider walking toward him. The dog held his breath. Pretending he did not see the gray wolf, Granite rested his head on his paws and shut his eyes. He hoped that Strider would pass by and curl up beside Roamer.

The ruse did not work. Granite heard a low whine. He opened an eye. In front of him stood Strider, his front paws nearly touching Granite's nose. Between his jaws was a large bone.

Granite laid back his ears and tried to squeeze

himself through the snow and into the ground beneath. Then he waited.

Strider did not go away. He looked straight at Granite, whined again, and dropped the bone in front of the dog. Then he wagged his tail. Without waiting for a response, he walked away.

Granite blinked in surprise. A surge of joy swept over him. Two summers had come and gone since he had joined the pack, and they were deep into another winter. All that time, Snowdrift's love had protected him, but he had remained an outsider. After such a long time, Granite was finally home.